Reaper's Jewels

by
Author Marissa Ann

Warning:
Credits:
Cover Design by: Francessca's PR & Designs
Editor: Rachel Goldman
Blurb: Melissa Mitchell

ASIN:
ISBN-13:   978-1-7365798-2-4

Author's Note

I want all my fans to know that I appreciate every single one of you! I couldn't do this without you! You all have made my dreams come true. Let me know what all you think of Reaper and Jade. I loved this couple so much!

To my husband: Thank you for always being there to listen when writing frustrates me beyond belief! You are always there to tell me that you have faith in what all I can do. I love you Ole Man! More than you'll ever know!

Prologue

Reaper

When a man makes a huge dumbass mistake when it comes to the woman he loves, the best thing he can do is force her back home until she forgives him. Right?

It's not like she is the only one with a reason to be pissed the fuck off. She ran off, had MY kid and was never planning to tell me about her. Yeah, I have a daughter now.

This changes things, it changes everything. I don't give a shit what I have to do, I'll pay every dime that weasel divorce lawyer is trying to get for that bitch I'm married to.

I should have done it three years ago and went after Jade when she left. But I didn't. It was the worst mistake of my life.

Hopefully Jade will forgive me for the last three years. Right now though I think she may want to kill me in my sleep. I didn't give her a choice about going back home.

Jade

He really thinks making me go back to North Mississippi against my will is going to help him win me back. He can go jump off the nearest cliff!

He didn't want me three years ago. He made that pretty damn plain. Especially when he allowed that bitch to talk to me as if I were just one of the whores that hangs around the club being passed around like a toy.

She had been gone for a couple years and everyone knew Reaper had filed for a divorce. I was so naive to think he was actually in love with me. After what happened that day and the way he acted like she was right about me being nothing to him, I know now, his feelings for me was not that deep.

I have no plans to forgive him. I know he only wants me now because we share a child. Family means everything to the Star family. And now our daughter is a part of that.

Chapter 1
Jade

"Finding anything?" My sister who likes to be called Fire these days asks as she takes the seat across from me.

There aren't very many customers inside the small restaurant this time of the day. I always loved it here before I moved away. Clyde's is the normal hang out of the older generation. They always tell the best stories of times past.

The waitress, Janice, is the same waitress that was working here three years ago. Not much changes in small towns.

"There are not many job openings here. I may need to go to the employment office and see what they can find for me." I put the paper down, picking up my coffee mug to finish it off.

"Will your savings be enough to keep you afloat until you find something here? You don't have rent or utilities to worry about." Fire has always looked out for me.

When our parents died, she did what she needed to in order to get the judge to sign off on giving her custody of me. I love her for all of it.

"It should. I don't like not paying you at least something for staying in the house."

"That house was left to both of us, Jade. Mom and Dad would want you there. I want you there." She frowns at me. "How did Amber act when you dropped her off at daycare this morning?"

"She was great. Talked the whole way there about all the friends she was going to make." I shake my head with a smile.

"She's a great kid. You've done well raising her by yourself the last three years. I'm sorry I missed most of it."

"That was mostly my fault. I shouldn't have run off like I did or made you swear not to tell anyone where I was." I reach over, grabbing her hand and squeeze it.

"You're family. The only one I really have. I will always do anything for you."

"What about Spark?" As soon as I ask, she pulls away. I can see her starting to clam up.

"What about him?" She huffs out.

"You two are still married." I look directly at her, willing her to talk about it.

"But we were never really married. We only did it so that I would have a better chance in court to get custody of you while you were still under age. We're just friends." She refuses to look me in the eye on the last part.

"I know for a fact, you have never wanted to just be his friend." I whisper across the table to her.

"Yeah, well, that's all he wants. So." She shrugs.

—

"If that's true, then why hasn't he filed for a divorce already? Hmm? I'm no longer under age. I haven't been in over three years."

She looks up at me quickly but doesn't respond back to what I said. I know my sister well enough to know that she'll think long and hard over my comments. Hopefully she'll realize that she should try hard to keep her marriage going. Neither one of them will go in the right direction without being pushed. They are both the most stubborn people I know.

"Well, I need to get to work. The paperwork at the garage has gotten behind since I was gone for so long. He doesn't even know how many log trailers they've sold in the past year. The CPA can't get the business taxes finished until I can give her an accounting of everything. I don't know why the asshat didn't just find someone else to take the job." Fire stands up from her chair.

"You know why, even if you don't want to admit it." I smile at the snarl on her face.

While both Reaper and Spark own the log trailer business called Hauler's, Spark is the one that runs the day to day business side. He would never allow Reaper to replace Fire with someone new.

The bell above the door jingles before Fire reaches it. Looking up I see Reaper walking in. The butterflies in my stomach go haywire from just looking at him. I see the two of them pass each other without a word as he heads in my direction.

"Your sister still has no manners I see." He comments as he takes the seat she just vacated.

"Neither do you. What are you doing here anyway?" My snarky side making an appearance.

"Just thought we could talk for a bit since you refused to move into my place. It would have made things easier."

"Are you still married?" I hold my back up straight already knowing his answer.

"You know that I technically am. I've been in the middle of a divorce since way before you ever left. You know that." He growls at me but I refuse to back down.

"The day I left it didn't sound like you were interested in a divorce after she mentioned her son possibly being yours. You very quickly threw away what we could have had by jumping at the chance that she may have been telling the truth." I can feel my own anger starting to service.

"I didn't find out until later that she was lying. You should have stayed!"

"For what? You stood there and told her I was nothing to you. That the two of you could raise the baby together, as a family. You threw me away like trash! I don't owe you a damn thing!" I yell at him as I push away from the table to leave.

Screw him! I think to myself as I walk out the door.

Reaper

After Jade left me in the restaurant, I decided to swing by the daycare center to check in on Amber. It still feels so alien to me that I am a father.

My soon to be ex was lying all those years ago about the baby boy she had given birth to. She had hoped that I wouldn't demand a DNA test. I almost didn't. The guys in my club finally talked some sense into my ass several months after Jade had already left.

I had been spiraling by then, constantly drinking. The guys wouldn't even let me work in the shop by that point. Looking back, I don't blame them. I could have gotten myself or any of them hurt. I would have hated myself for that.

Spark finally got enough of my bullshit, getting the guys together to either straighten me out or beat the hell out of me.

I stopped drinking to excess after that, only having a few beers with the guys a few times a month. Now, I mostly just go home to my huge empty house alone.

Except Spark is there, which makes no sense to me. He's in love with his wife Fire. Always has been even though he still refuses to admit it. Both of them are too stubborn to see what everyone else already sees.

Walking into the daycare, I'm hit with the smell of crayons and baby powder.

"Reaper, what are you doing here?" Mrs. Morris asks from the front desk.

"I just wanted to check on Amber. Make sure she is adjusting to her first day."

"She's doing just fine. They are in the room coloring right now. Would you like to go back and see her?"

"Nah, that's okay. I'll see her later after her mom picks her up." I'm still nervous to be around her without Jade being around.

It's why I think we need to sit down for a serious conversation. I'm not even sure what, if anything, she has told Amber about her father.

"If she needs anything though, please call me down at the shop. I'll make sure she has it."

After Mrs. Morris promises that she will, I leave and head towards my lawyers office. It's time something was done about my divorce.

Jade

I walked down to the little park in town to cool off after getting so pissed off at Reaper. He has no right to make any kind of demands. My life has been fine without him. I'm no longer a naive teenager with stars in her eyes when looking at him. But damn, looking at him still causes butterflies.

I'm lost in thoughts of the past as I sit on the bench not noticing the people that are coming and going until I hear someone calling my name.

"Jade, is that you?" Looking up I see Jaymie Wilson. We went to school together. He was always a good looking guy, even asked me to prom although I turned him down. I was too in love with Reaper at the time.

"Hey! Long time no see!" I smile when he walks up to hug me.

"Damn girl. Where have you been? All anyone would say was that you left but they would never say where." He sits down next to me on the bench with a smile.

"I was in New Orleans taking some classes. I have a daughter now."

"Yeah, I heard about the daughter. News of that got around town pretty quick. Small town life hasn't changed since you've been gone." He laughs.

"That doesn't surprise me. What about you? I figured you'd have moved away by now. You used to talk about getting away as soon as graduation was over."

"I'm actually finishing up a business degree. My Uncle is hoping that I will take over the hardware store. That's actually where I am headed now. There's a girl that is supposed to interview for a sales clerk position."

"Does the store have an open position? I didn't see it in the paper this morning when I was looking at available jobs." I ask excitedly while hoping he's not yet set to hire this other girl.

"Uh Yeah. I didn't realize you were looking for one. I just assumed that Reaper would be taking care of everything since you are back." He looks at me with interest.

"Absolutely not. Why would he? We are not together regardless of what you may have heard." I answer with a slight anger to my voice.

"I didn't mean any disrespect, Jade. I'm sorry. Look, why don't you come to the store with me and you can fill out an application? It would be nice to hire someone I actually know." He smiles a megawatt smile at me.

"Sounds like a plan." I smile back, standing up to walk with him.

"Do you think we could maybe go get dinner one night?" He looks directly at me and I know he's asking for a real date.

"That actually sounds nice. I'd love to." I answer with a smile.

Reaper

Immersing myself into work hoping it'll make the time go by faster, I don't realize it's lunch time until Grease hits the back of my welding helmet and I turn off the welder.

"Dude! Take a break. You've been going nonstop since you got here this morning. I ordered burgers." He holds up the bags of food that he had delivered.

"Let me wash up and I'll meet you in the office." I say as I take off my gloves.

"I'll grab some water bottles from the cooler." He says over his shoulder as he walks away.

Getting back to the office a few minutes later, I find Grease slouched back in a chair in front of my desk with his feet up.

"Just make yourself at home." I growl.

"I will." He smiles before taking a huge bite from his burger. I just shake my head at him as I sit down behind my desk.

We eat in silence for several minutes, enjoying the coolness of the air conditioning. My mind is still on what I found out from my lawyer.

I married Brandi when I was only seventeen years old. She had convinced me to run off to Alabama and get married in the courthouse there. All I can say now is that it was the biggest, dumbest mistake ever.

By doing it that way, there was no prenuptial agreement in place to protect the interests of the businesses that my parents had started that they planned to leave to us kids. Each of us Star kids are worth a couple million each even though you can't tell by how we live our lives.

Brandi's lawyer of course was able to get all of my financial records when we started divorce proceedings. Now, the two of them are trying to get as much as possible and I am fighting to give them as little as possible.

It's been a long messy divorce that has ruined several things in my life including losing the one that I truly love.

"Seen your girl earlier." Grease says, breaking my brooding silence.

"She was at Clyde's this morning looking at job listings in the paper." I murmur.

"Nah, man, I didn't see her at Clyde's. She was at the hardware store. It looked like she was putting in an application but it also looked like Jay was being extra friendly." He wags his eyebrows up and down.

"What do you mean extra friendly?" My eyes narrow at the thoughts running through my head.

"I overheard them talking about going to dinner together this weekend. Neither of them realized I was even in the store. They moved to the office after that, so I don't know all the plans."

"Like hell she's going on a date!" I growl.

"Why can't she?" I hear from the door. Looking up I see Fire standing there.

"Is she just going to leave Amber with a sitter?" I snarl. Fire has always brought out the worst in me.

Back when Jade first left, Fire found me at the old cabin I own in the middle of three hundred acres. I was drunk off my ass, as naked as the day I was born but she thought setting fire to the old ramshackle cabin would be amusing. She's the sister of the woman I love, my sister in law by marriage but I swear the woman is the devil incarnate.

"If she needs a sitter, I would be more than happy to baby-sit my own niece while Jade goes out for some fun. Besides, she's too young to be alone forever." Fire smiles evilly at me knowing just what to say to get under my skin.

"Why are you in here anyway besides to torment me?" I finally ask with a calmer voice.

"Some of the files in my office are missing some invoices that I need to put into the computer. Thought I would see if they were in here."

"In the bottom drawer of the black filing cabinet." I point to the one I'm talking about. I watch as she gets the files from the corner of my eye and starts back out the door but stops to look back at me.

"You know, if you want her back you might want to learn to control your temper and perhaps.., this is only a suggestion, but do things a bit different than you normally would." With that, she leaves my office.

What kind of different? I think to myself.

Chapter 2
Jade

Getting the job at the hardware store put a new spring into my step. I've never been the type to sit around and do nothing. While my parents left us a hefty inheritance, I've never wanted to spend a dime of it. It has always somehow felt wrong to do so.

When I finally figure out what it is that I really want to do, maybe I'll use part of it. Only thing I have ever really wanted to do was raise horses.

Jay put me straight to work the very same day that I filled out the application and I've had a full schedule ever since.

He and I have talked quite a bit while at work. He's still the easy going guy that I knew from school. Tonight he's taking me on our first date. I'd be lying if I said I wasn't nervous.

Since I turned fifteen years old I've only ever thought about Reaper. I tried to date a couple years ago not long after Amber was born. I broke it off with the guy a few weeks later. Besides, he hated the fact I always had to make plans around being able to get a babysitter. If you don't have time for my daughter, then you don't have time for me.

"Are you sure you are okay with her for tonight? I would think you had plans or something." I ask Fire again as I walk into the living room.

"We will be fine. Besides, I like being back home." Fire says from the couch where she is sharing a bowl of popcorn with Amber.

I hear a knock at the door and know that it is Jay.

"Hey, Jade?" I look back at Fire. "Have fun tonight okay? You deserve it." She says.

"I plan to!" I laugh before opening the door.

It's time that I got back into life. Pining over Reaper is behind me. He's part of my past even though he will always be in my life because we share a daughter. That doesn't mean he gets to rule my life.

Reaper

I know from Spark that Jade went on that date tonight with that asshole Jay. Although I can secretly admit that he's a nice guy except for the fact he's trying to take my girl.

She's been mine since I stopped long enough to really notice her on her sixteenth birthday. The way that she looked at me then drove me crazy waiting around for her to be of legal age.

I wish she still looked at me that way now instead of the hate I see flaring into her eyes every time she looks at me.

I'm sitting here on my front porch currently brooding while all the guys hang out around the fire pit in the yard.

Our clubhouse is about a mile from here but other than some of the guys having rooms there, we all hang out here. We are so very different from most clubs as we have been semi-legit for years making most of our money the legal way.

Doesn't mean that we have gone soft though. We would all still kill if it meant protecting each other or our families.

"Brooding again?" Spark asks, taking a seat on the porch steps.

"Does it look like it?" I snarl, downing my beer. It's my first and most likely my only one for the night since I mostly quit.

"Have the two of you had a chance to sit and talk yet?" He asks, referring to Jade and I.

"It turns into a huge argument two point six seconds into the conversation." I sigh, running my hand over my face.

"Maybe you should try tying her to a chair with a gag over her mouth. That's what I've imagined doing to Fire several times. It might work." Spark says with seriousness but I just laugh at him.

"You and Fire were made for each other, man. Hard Headed as hell, mouthy and blood thirsty too." I shake my head at him. "Where is your wife tonight anyway?"

"Babysitting Amber while Jade is out on her date."

He waits for my explosion but all I can do is grit my teeth. I currently have no right to claim Jade, which pisses me the hell off. Standing up, I grab my keys, heading down the porch steps.

"Where you going?" Spark asks.

"To scare away a mouse!" I growl.

"No way am I going to miss this!" Spark laughs.

"Me either!" Grease steps out from the shadows of the house. I should have known he was there. He's never far from my side, always there to watch over me as he's done since my parents passed away.

"Tell Loki we'll be back later and to be sure the rest of these fuck heads don't burn my fucking house down." I direct Grease who immediately goes in search of Loki.

We call him that because the fucker is always pulling pranks on the other guys. Sometimes pushing the limits too far. More than once I've kept some of the guys from literally killing his ass.

I don't wait for Grease and Spark before pulling out of the driveway. Those two fuckers won't be far behind me anyway.

That little shithead Jay has been after my girl since they were both in school together. It was made clear to him back then that she was off limits. I guess he needs a new reminder. I'm going to make sure he fucking gets it.

Jade

By the end of dinner, I knew that this with Jay would never work. There is absolutely no spark between us. At least there isn't for me.

I spent most of the night comparing him to Reaper, just like I did the few other times I tried to date someone after having Amber.

I'll never get Reaper out of my system. I still want him but the fucker is going to have to work for it.

"Thank you for dinner. I had a really nice time." I say to Jay as we pull up to the house.

"It was nice. I get the feeling though that from now on it'll be just friends?" He asks with a smile.

"I'm sorry." I give a small smile with my apology.

"There's no reason to be sorry. You've been in love with Reaper since we were kids. I get it." He gets a faraway look in his eyes.

"Something tells me there's a story there. Want to talk about it?" I reach over and put my hand on his arm.

"Not really. Goodnight Jade." He lifts my hand from his arm kissing the back of it.

"Goodnight." I say as I get out of the car.

He waits until I get my front door unlocked before driving away. Always a gentleman.

Walking in, I find Fire and Amber asleep on the couch. Deciding not to disturb them, I head to my room to get ready for bed.

Reaper

I'm sitting on his porch swing in the shadows when he pulls up. Spark and Grease are around somewhere.

When we got here, I told the two of them to stay out of the way and let me take care of this. It's my business, not club business. They of course argued about that saying that being the Prez, everything I do is club business. They have a point but I don't need their interference in this.

He gets all the way to the door before he sees me sitting in the swing.

"I figured you'd show up." He laughs a little as he walks over.

"She's still my girl." I growl.

"More than you know actually." He smiles again.

"What do you mean?" I ask with interest.

"We are only friends, Jade and I. Just as we were in high school. Even so, she still sees herself as yours. Although I think you have your work cut out for you on making things right." He sits in the chair next to the swing, looking at me.

"I've got to get that stupid bitch to sign those divorce papers." I scrub my hands over my face.

"You definitely need to do that but you also need to romance Jade. Get her to see that she is what's most important to you." He states matter of factly.

"She's always been the most important thing in the world to me." I growl at him.

"You chose Brandi over her, man. Don't say you didn't because everyone knows that you did. All because you thought her child was yours and you have some old fashioned bullshit in your head about parents needing to be together for the kid." He shakes his head at me.

"Better watch yourself Jay." I growl. I can see Spark and Grease stepping out from the corner of the house. Jay sees them too but it doesn't seem to phase him.

"You're only getting mad because you know it's true." He huffs, sitting back into the chair. "Rough me up if you guys want to but it doesn't change the facts."

"What facts would that be?" I ask although I am sure I already know the answer.

"That sometimes the truth is hard to hear. Sometimes it hurts like hell but we all need people around us to pound that truth into our heads." He says.

"We've been trying for the past several years but Reaper here seems to have a head made of stone." Grease murmurs making Spark and Jay laugh.

"If you guys are done, I'm going in. I have an early finance class in the morning." Jay yawns.

"Yeah, we best get back and make sure the other guys haven't burned anything down." I step down off the porch as he heads towards his door. "Thanks Jay." I say before he walks inside.

"For what?" He asks.

"For being her friend." I say as I walk away.

I send the guys back to the house to check on everything as I make a detour that takes me by Jade's house.

Cutting the motor off, I walk my bike down the road so I don't wake up Jade and especially her sister. My fire breathing sister in law is likely to shoot my ass.

Leaving my bike at the curb, I walk around to the window that I know is Jade's room. It's open just a few inches letting in the breeze.

She makes a noise as I start to turn away. I realize that she is dreaming and talking in her sleep. I strain my ears to hear what she is mumbling. A few seconds later what I hear makes my cock start to rise.

"Please Reaper..." She moans the same way she did all those years ago when I made love to her in my bed.

This is a dream that I wish I could see, be a part of. Not wanting to be a sadistic fuck and continue to listen to her, I turn back towards my bike.

—

It's time for a cold ass shower. If that doesn't work, I can easily remember her soft heat as I jerk one out.

Chapter 3
Jade

Surprisingly, I've not seen much of Reaper for the past week. He worked out a schedule with me through text so that he can spend some time with our daughter which has started to make me feel left out.

I have no right to feel that way but he seemed like he wanted me back at first. Now it feels like he's given up on that.

I'm feeling really down by the time Thursday rolls around, that when I get a text from him, it surprises me.

Reaper: Will you have dinner with me tonight?

Jade: Sure. But I'll need to get a sitter.

Reaper: There's no need. Spark and Jade are going to take her to a movie.

Jade: Okay.

I wait a few minutes to see if he texts again. I'm truly surprised he'd already worked out someone to watch Amber.

Jade: Where are we going?

Reaper: Thought I'd cook us a couple steaks. Be at the house around 7pm?

The thought of being alone with him in his house causes several different emotions. If he were to touch me, I'd probably melt into a puddle on the floor.

Jade: I'll be there.

Reaper: Great! See you then!

The rest of the day seems to drag by. Getting off work at four, I head home to get ready. It takes longer than expected to finally decide on what to wear.

I don't want to wear something super sexy that would make him think he can just have me but I don't want to wear baggy clothes that would turn him off either.

Settling on a pair of shorts and a tank top, I put on just a little bit of makeup before I head out the door.

My stomach is doing somersaults by the time I pull up to his house. I stay sitting in my car for several minutes to control my breathing before I get out.

Walking up the steps, the door opens before I get to the top. Looking up, my breath leaves my body as I lay eyes on his completely naked chest that is only covered by tattoos.

I realize he's gotten quite a few more since I saw him naked last and wonder where else he may have gotten some. My nipples harden at the thought of exploring his body.

"Hello beautiful." He murmurs, drawing my eyes to his. I realize he knows exactly what I've been looking at. He probably even knows what I was thinking from the grin he's currently giving me.

"Hi." I say simply, straightening my shoulders.

"Come on in." He whispers huskily as I walk through the door he's holding open. "Steaks are almost done. I was just finishing up our salads."

I follow him into the kitchen to see that he was in the middle of chopping the vegetables. Taking a seat at the bar, I look around as he works noticing the newer touches he's added to the kitchen.

"I like the new cabinets." I say as I look over the details etched into the doors.

"Thanks. I found a guy in Kentucky that could create what I wanted. We just installed them last year." He explains.

"They are really nice. Did you ever get the master bathroom finished?" I ask curiously.

"Complete with a Jacuzzi tub." He grins mischievously. I can feel the heat collect into my cheeks. "Want to sit on the back deck while we eat?"

"That would be nice. Do the deer still come out into the field late in the evening?" I ask when we walk outside.

He grabs our steaks from the grill, placing them on our plates before sitting down.

"They do sometimes. There's a doe that comes in more often than the others with a couple babies. I like to sit out here and watch them play."

We eat mostly in silence, only making small talk here and there. I help him to clean up the kitchen afterwards.

"I told my lawyer to give Brandi whatever she wants. Whatever will get her to sign those fucking papers as soon as possible." He says as I put away the last plate after drying it.

"I'm not sure that this is any of my business." I turn to look at him, heart racing.

"You don't think it's any of your business? Everything I do is your business." He says with a sigh.

"You made your choice." I whisper.

As soon as my words are out, he crowds me against the counter, my breathing kicking up a notch.

"I made the gravest mistake of my life. I thought at the time I was doing what was right. I now know that being with someone just because of a child is not the right way to do things. It won't hold a marriage together." He breathes the words into my ear.

The closeness of his body against mine, causing my nipples to harden inside of my shirt. I push forward just to feel a little friction against them as my need to be touched heightens.

His lips on the shell of my ear open slightly as his tongue sweeps out to lick. Chill bumps cover my arms at the touch.

"Reaper, please." I beg, unsure if I'm begging for his touch or for him to stop.

He pushes his lower body farther into me. I can feel every inch of him against my core that becomes slick with a pulsing need.

"You are mine, Jade. You always have been, just as I have always been yours. I'm willing to wait for you to remember that." He whispers, rubbing himself into me one last time before moving back, putting distance between us.

My breathing is labored, my clit throbbing with want as I stare into his beautiful eyes. I want him but I need him to make me a priority in his life. His first thought no matter the circumstance.

"I think I should go now." I look away, grabbing my purse from the chair.

Thinking to get out the door before I throw caution to the wind and let him take me on the floor, I walk towards the front of the house. I'm almost out the door when he grabs me, turning me around into his arms.

His mouth lands on mine quickly, taking control. I immediately give in, touching my tongue to his. It ends almost as quickly as it began.

"I'll see you tomorrow." He whispers, looking into my eyes. I can only nod my head, not entirely sure what he's talking about.

My head is spinning too much for me to find out at the moment. I've got to get out of here so that I can think more clearly.

He doesn't say anything else or stop me again as I walk out. He just stands on the front porch watching as I leave down the driveway in my car.

Reaper

I've had a non-stop hard-on since Jade left earlier after our dinner. Her response to me has given me new hope for our future.

I'm watching a movie when Spark finally gets home, plopping down in the other recliner.

"Long night little brother?" I ask, looking at his pissed off look.

"It was a great night. At least it was until about thirty minutes ago." He sighs.

"What happened? Fire try to kill you?" I laugh.

"She actually did. At least I thought she was going to kill me. She only held back because Amber was in the house." He grumbles.

Having my full attention now, I look over at him to see if he's bleeding anywhere. Can't be too careful where my sister in law is concerned.

"So what happened?" I ask.

"I asked her when she wanted to file divorce papers." He looks over at me in confusion as I start laughing so hard tears come into my eyes.

"Why are you laughing?" He growls, throwing a magazine at my head.

"Because you two are blind as damn bats, man. Seriously!" I calm myself from laughing enough to tell him.

"What the fuck are you talking about?" He looks at me waiting for an explanation.

"You stupid ass! She's just as much in love with you as you are with her! Of course she got pissed off with you asking about a divorce." I shake my head at him.

"We only got married so that the judge would let her raise Jade instead of putting her in foster care. She even reminded me that's why we were getting married the day we went to the courthouse!" He yells.

"You are blinded by what she has said. You need to step back and look at it all with new eyes. I'm telling you, your wife is in love with you. Don't let the woman you want go so easily. First thing you need to do is never ever mention divorce to her again. Don't you think if she wanted one, she'd have filed four years ago when Jade turned eighteen?" I watch as my words start to sink in with him.

After a few minutes, he gets a silly grin on his face before he gets up from the recliner.

"Where you off to now?" I ask.

"I need some sleep. Little Amber has more energy than I have ever had. We took her to the arcade at the mall after the movie. She was determined to play every single one. I'm beat!" I laugh at his explanation.

Heading to bed myself a few minutes later, I lay there awake thinking of Jade. The way she felt against my body in the kitchen. I need her like I need the air to breathe.

―

My cock hardens in my boxers I wore to bed. Turning onto my stomach, I push into the mattress hoping it'll go down on it's own. It doesn't. It only makes it worse.

Turning back over, I reach down grabbing myself. Closing my eyes, I imagine Jade with her legs wrapped around me as I hold her up by her thighs.

Remembering what her heat felt like as my cock rocked in and out of her, I begin to stroke myself. I'm so close to coming already, I know that only a few more strokes of my hand will push me over.

The second I think of her moaning my name the way she did the night I looked into her window, I come all at once. My boxers catching most of it before it got on the sheets.

A few minutes later, I get up, cleaning myself off as I climb back into bed. I fall asleep quickly only to wake up a few hours later with my cock hard as a rock again from dreaming about her.

I might die from jerking off to her before I again experience the real thing. However, I'm hopeful that she gives in sooner rather than later.

She really does mean the world to me. I need her to forget about my stupid mistake and give me another chance to prove it.

Jade

Fire was more than pissed off by the time I made it home. I was currently waiting for her to calm down enough to tell me what happened. From her current ramblings I can tell it is definitely Spark's fault.

"So, what did Spark do?" I calmly ask.

"He asked me about filing for a divorce! A divorce, Jade!" She sits ramrod straight, trying to hold back the tears I know are lurking in her eyes.

"He said he was filing for a divorce?" I ask, trying to find out exactly how bad this was.

"No. He asked me when I was going to file for one!" I can tell that my sister is truly upset so I try not to let her see my half smile.

"Sweetheart, you are only looking at this from one side. Did it ever occur to you that maybe he was asking to see how you feel about it all?" I gently ask.

"What do you mean?" She looks at me curiously.

"If he actually wanted a divorce, don't you think he'd have gotten one by now?" I wait for her to process that.

"He doesn't see me as anything more than a friend, Jade. He never has!" Her shoulders slump at her statement.

"I think you are wrong about that. You might want to start making your feelings known, Fire. Before it's too late." I leave her sitting on the couch as I head to bed.

Chapter 4
Reaper

Last night with Jade gave me a renewed hope that we can get back to the way it should have always been between the two of us.

Walking into the shop the next morning, I see that most of the guys are already here finishing up the welds that were needed on a log trailer that came in earlier in the week.

It had been in a wreck that bent several of the standards in the middle. The standards are what keep the logs in place. If they are not straight, it could cause logs to fall while being transported down the highway.

"Is it almost ready to be picked up?" I ask Spark as I walk around double checking the work my guys did.

I have complete faith in the work my guys do. They are the best in the industry as far as I have seen. We do quality work very quickly here at Hauler's. People come from several states away to buy a new trailer we have made or to have us fix one they already own.

"It should be ready to go by this afternoon." Spark says.

"I'll give Mr. Dave a call and see if he needs it transported or if one of his guys will be picking it up." I state as I head towards the office to do just that.

After taking care of the business side of things, I wonder briefly about asking Jade to supper again but this time with Amber in mind as well.

I quickly send a text asking her if we can take Amber to get Pizza tomorrow night together. In my mind it will be a family outing and I need Jade to start seeing us as a family unit.

It doesn't take but a few minutes before she replies back that Amber would enjoy that. She doesn't say anything else but I am hoping that Jade will enjoy it as well.

I will break down her walls she has built up against me little by little.

Jade

When Reaper asked about us taking Amber to get pizza, I tried to not let my heart flutter over the thought of him wanting to spend more time with me even with our daughter in tow.

We decided that Amber and I would just meet him there since I would already be in town after working and picking up Amber from the daycare.

Walking inside to pick up Amber, I see that most of the kids have already been picked up for the day.

Amber is in the back of the class sitting with a cute little boy. She's just talking away to him while he sits quietly watching her.

"Hello, Jade." Mrs. Morris says after she spots me walking into the room.

"Hey, Mrs. Morris. Who is the little boy with Amber?" I ask, still watching the two interact.

"Um, well, that is Cole Halloway. Brandi Halloway's son." Mrs. Morris says quietly.

Everyone in town knows my history along with Reaper's. Brandi is Reaper's ex-wife and Cole is the child she tried to pass off as being Reaper's.

"Him and Amber are friends then?" I ask.

"Surprisingly, yes. You may not know this but Cole is different from the other children.

He has never spoken a single word. And until your sweet girl started school here, I have never seen him smile." She says as we watch Amber, still talking non-stop to Cole who smiles at something she just said.

I am super proud of my daughter at this moment. She picked the shyest kid in class who probably doesn't have many friends to befriend. I can't help but smile.

We leave soon after, mostly because I wanted to be gone before Brandi finally remembered to pick Cole up. I had rather not run into her in public.

Our night out with Reaper goes smoothly. To watch Amber and her father laugh and play, I wonder what I was thinking by not telling him about my pregnancy as soon as I found out. He's an amazing dad, always so patient with her even when she asks the same exact question fifty different ways.

Back at home while in bed, I think about the kiss he gave me as we left the pizza place. I really shouldn't have allowed such a kiss but it's hard to deny what my body wants.

Thinking of him now, I feel my core becoming slick with my own juices as my clit throbs for attention.

Reaching down, I glide two fingers into my wetness, rubbing circles into my clit and can't hold back the sigh that escapes my lips.

My other hand slides up my stomach until it reaches my nipple and I give it a squeeze. My core tightens up letting me know how truly close I am to an orgasm.

I quicken the pace of my fingers circling my clit, pinching my nipple at the same time as I think about Reaper's hard body against mine.

Although I feel the edge of my orgasm, I can't get myself to fall over the cliff. I need more, so I push my two fingers into my slit as I pinch my nipple even harder. The second I think of Reaper's eyes, I'm moaning out my orgasm as my insides clench down on my fingers.

I'll never be able to resist him. I think later as I lay in bed after cleaning myself up.

Reaper

"What do you mean she's out of town and can't come to the meeting? Surely you told her I am willing to give her whatever as long as she signs these fucking papers?" I growl across the table at Brandi's lawyer.

"She does realize that, Mr. Star but she had a family emergency to come up." He explains calmly.

"It's okay Reaper, we will reschedule and we will get everything done." My lawyer tries to placate me but all I do is stand up and leave the office.

This shit with her is getting old. There is always some excuse to not show up for meetings or court hearings. She just plans to always make my life a living hell.

Getting back to the shop, I immerse myself in work to drown out all thoughts of the bitch that has done everything possible to destroy my life.

At the end of the day, I have everything worked out for the trailers that are ready to be picked up or delivered. Those will bring in a good income for the boys and myself.

We also have a large pay day coming up from a shipment that Chucky along with a few of our other guys will go pick up from Florida later this week.

With most of the states leaning more towards legalization of marijuana, we may need to reevaluate the clubs future business plans.

I didn't plan anything with Jade and Amber tonight so I plan to go straight home and crash. I'm mentally tired and need the rest after today.

Tomorrow though, I will contact Jade and see if we can make plans. I don't intend to give her much time away from me in the coming weeks. I want my girl back. Completely.

Chapter 5
Reaper

The next couple of weeks fly by as Jade and I get into the habit of planning things together. I always make sure that I find small reasons to touch her in some way, wanting her to be as affected as I am by her.

Making sure that I'm around a lot has been effective in establishing a connection with my daughter. She seems to take things in stride and didn't even take time to think before calling me daddy.

The very first time she did, I had to turn away so that she wouldn't see the tears in my eyes. Her mother saw them though, giving me a sad smile as she mouthed I'm sorry yet again.

I no longer blame her for what she did. I even understand it. She was hurt and by the time she found out she was pregnant with Amber, that hurt had started to turn into something else. She also didn't want to be the other woman.

Jade and I had a movie night planned for tonight so I leave work early to pick up our supper on the way to the house.

Right around the time she's supposed to be here, there's a knock on the door. Thinking it's her, I swing the door open ready to demand why she didn't just use the key I had given her just last week.

Standing in the door though is Brandi. Before I can say anything she holds her hands up to stop me.

"I'm sorry to just show up but I really need to talk to you." Just as she finishes, Jade's car pulls up.

My heart runs crazy expecting her to fly off the handle and think I've messed up again. Instead, she slowly gets out of the car, looks at us standing on the porch and walks up to us.

"Brandi." She says quietly as she wraps her arm around my waist. Pride swarms my chest as I wrap my arm back around her.

"Hello, Jade. I heard you were back in town." Surprisingly, Brandi isn't at all condescending or rude which is completely unlike her. "I need to talk to the two of you for a few minutes if that's okay?" While the question is directed to both of us, she looks to Jade for an answer.

"Sure, come on in." Jade extends the invite.

Although I don't want her in my house, I allow Jade to lead Brandi into the kitchen to take a seat at the table. I sit next to Jade and wait for Brandi to explain what the hell she wants.

"I'm willing to sign your divorce papers without taking a single dime of your money." Brandi blurts out suddenly.

"Why? What else are you wanting?" I growl, afraid of what it is.

——

"Reaper, give her a chance." Jade whispers, trying to calm me.

"Her? You know her as well as I do, Jade. She wants something. Bad enough that she's willing to forego a hell of a lot of money. So what is it that you are wanting?" I hold my breath, looking directly at the bitch that has made my life a living hell since I was sixteen years old.

"I want the two of you to take Cole." She states simply.

Cole is the son she had claimed was mine. The DNA test that I finally had run proved that he wasn't.

"Why?" Jade asks, just as confused as I am.

"I can't take care of him any more. While I am sure that most people, especially the two of you, think that I am a heartless bitch, I do care about Cole. As much as I can care about someone." She pushes her shoulders back at her admission.

"Why can't you take care of him any more?" Jade asks with sympathy. My girl has a heart of gold, even to those that do her wrong. It makes my heart swell even more.

"He hasn't spoken yet. Not a single word. Loves to just sit by himself. I took him to some doctors down in Jackson. They say he's most likely on the spectrum. That he'll need all this extra help. I only got pregnant on purpose as a way to try to keep you Reaper. We all know that already. But there is no way that I can take care of a child that can't do things for himself. I have plans for my life that don't include all kinds of doctor's appointments. Besides, I'm seeing someone." Brandi explains.

"What about the real father? Can't he help you?" I ask through gritted teeth. I always knew she wasn't the mother type, I just wish I hadn't been blinded to it before we were married.

"I honestly don't know who he is." She admits without looking at us. "Will the two of you at least think about it? I know the two of you would be great parents to him. You'd give him everything he would ever need. Something that I can never do." She actually has real tears in her eyes when she finishes speaking.

"We'll talk it over. Can we maybe call you in a few days and let you know?" Jade asks, reaching out to touch Brandi on the arm surprising her.

"Please do. Here is my cell number. I'd like to get this done sooner rather than later. I'm supposed to meet my boyfriend down in Florida later next week. If you two don't want him, I'm going to contact family services." Brandi states, getting up from the table and leaving out the door. A few minutes later we hear her car leaving the driveway.

—

"Well, I wasn't expecting that when I pulled up to see the two of you on the porch." Jade laughs a little.

"I wasn't expecting that when I found her on the doorstep either. You think it's something we should actually think about instead of just telling her no?" I ask, unsure of what Jade is thinking.

"Have you seen him lately? Cole, I mean?" She asks.

"No. I've not seen him since he was around one years old I think. Why?" Not sure where she's going with this.

"He goes to daycare with Amber. Mrs. Morris said that Amber sits with him every single day and seems to know what he wants without him ever making a sound. She said she's never seen him smile before Amber started to school there. He now smiles, every single day. So do I think it would be worth talking about? I do." She smiles waiting for my response.

"Then how about we run by my lawyer's office in the morning and see what he has to say about it?" I ask, smiling back as she hugs me.

"Do you think you could love a child that's not yours just as much as one that is?" She pulls back, looking into my eyes.

"Are you asking if I can love one that's not mine or if I can love one that is hers?" I ask seriously.

"Both?" She whispers.

"Technically he would be ours as soon as the papers are signed, therefore yes, I will love him just as much as I love Amber." I pull her into my lap, loving the closeness we have settled into.

Hopefully soon, I can have her even closer. In my bed and eventually living in this house with me.

Jade

Reaper and I have been taking things slow. Having date nights with him has been worth looking forward to.

When I arrived earlier and found Brandi standing on the front porch with him, I got scared at first of what was going on. Going with my gut, I walked up anyway. My nerves settled once he put his arm around me.

What she's asking from us is a big commitment on our part. It's kind of surprising that she would think of the two of us as the best fit for her child. I admire that she acknowledges the fact of her limited mothering skills. At least she cares enough about him to want him to have better than she can provide.

The fact that Reaper is willing to consider it causes my heart to swell with pride. He's willing to forgive enough to take the woman's child as his own. I love him even more for that.

Sitting in his lap earlier started a need inside of me that I don't think I can deny tonight.

Currently curled up together on the large sofa watching a movie, I push my rear into him as my hand rubs softly up his thigh. It doesn't take but a minute until I feel his hot breath next to my ear.

"Careful, Jade, I can only hold back for so long." He whispers as he pushes his now hard cock into my backside.

"I don't want you to hold back." I whisper back.

Turning to face him, I run my hands under his shirt across his stomach. He growls at my touch, taking me into a deep breathtaking kiss.

I climb on top of him to straddle his waist, fitting my core more tightly to him. I make myself moan from the contact.

Without breaking our kiss, he gets up from the sofa, carrying me up the stairs to the master bedroom. Sitting me on the side of the bed, he pulls my shirt over my head revealing my lacey bra.

He watches my eyes as I reach behind me, undoing the clasp setting my breasts free.

"Fuck, beautiful." He whispers just before pulling my right nipple into his mouth.

I fall back on the bed with a moan as he sucks harder at my nipple, grazing it with his teeth. I feel my core tighten at what's to come.

"I need more." I moan as he moves to the other nipple.

Reaching between us, he unbuttons my jeans. As he kisses a line down my stomach, he slowly pulls my jeans down my legs taking my panties with them. Instead of taking them completely off, he leaves them at my knees making it impossible to spread my legs.

"You smell so good." I can feel his breath on my clit as he rubs his nose along my slit.

"Play with those nipples for me baby." He commands, my hands moving to squeeze my own nipples.

Never losing eye contact, his tongue slips out of his mouth to push against my clit but doesn't move.

"Please, Reaper." I beg but he still doesn't move. Looking into his eyes, I finally realize what he's waiting for. "Please, Rafe, I need you." I breathe out heavily.

He immediately sucks my clit into his mouth, rubbing his tongue over it rapidly. My core tightens up with an impending release that is long overdue. Within moments, I scream out my release.

He continues to stroke my body as I come down from the high he just took me on. Kissing up my body until his eyes are even with my own.

"Still the most beautiful thing I have ever seen." He whispers, kissing my ear.

"My turn." I whisper, pushing him onto his back.

Quickly taking my clothes the rest of the way off, I push his shirt up over his head only to his elbows so his arms can't move. I nibble at his own nipples, making him moan. I smile at the sound, moving down along his stomach until I get to his jeans.

Slowly pulling his jeans down only until his cock pops free, I lick my tongue up the side from the base to the tip.

"Fuck, baby." He strains out.

I cup his balls in one hand, gently squeezing until he looks down into my eyes. I then, slowly suck the tip of his cock into my mouth going down ever so slowly. I feel his cock jerk at the contact and he moans.

I slowly build up to a pace that is comfortable for my mouth. I can feel him getting closer to release but he's still holding back.

Grabbing his thigh with my other hand, I dig my nails into him. Within seconds he is coming into my mouth with a roar. I swallow him down until he is completely spent before releasing his shaft from my mouth with a pop.

"Holy fuck! That was hot as hell!" He breathes out hard as I climb up his body to lay next to him.

Reaper

Jade and I lay snuggled together on the couch for a while. We must both fall into sleep because I jerk awake to the sound of my phone buzzing on the floor.

Reaching for it, I can see it's a text from Grease that says to call him. I look to see what time it is and I'm surprised that it's midnight.

"I should go." Jade murmurs as my movements woke her up.

"You could just stay." I whisper, striking her face with my hand.

"I don't want Amber to wake up and I'm not there." She says reasonably.

I don't argue the point because our daughter comes first. Next time though, I will make sure she brings Amber with her. She has her own room upstairs that I fixed up for her as soon as we got back home weeks ago.

I walk her outside, kissing her hard on the porch and wait until her tail lights can no longer be seen before I go back inside to call Grease.

"Hey man, didn't mean to bother you tonight but there's a slight issue." He says as soon as he picks up.

"It's okay brother, what's up?"

"Some kids broke into the shop and trashed the place. Don't think they were trying to steal anything, just looking to be a couple jackasses." He huffs.

"Are the cops there?" I ask, rubbing my face.

"Haven't called them yet, wanted to talk to you first. I have them both here in the office with me now." He growls out.

I smile at the thought of them being scared to death of Grease. If you don't know him well, you'd be intimidated by him too.

"Stay right there. I'll be there in twenty." I say, hanging up the phone.

Exactly twenty minutes later, I pull up to the shop. I can clearly see the damage they did to the front door to get in as I walk inside.

"Prez." Grease greets me as I walk into the office, taking a seat behind the desk.

I eye the two boys sitting on the couch. Both sit staring at the ground in front of them.

"You two seem to have too much time on your hands. What exactly were you trying to accomplish by breaking in? Grease here says you weren't stealing anything. Is that true?" I demand answers from them both.

"We just wanted to look around, sir." The one on the right answers.

"If all you wanted to do was look around, then why does my shop look like a tornado hit it?" I growl, watching him squirm. "Maybe I should call the cops and let them handle the two of you." I sit back with a sigh.

"No, please. We can clean it up. I promise we can. Right Carter?" The one on the right answers, nudging his quiet friend on the left.

"So his name is Carter, what's yours?" I ask.

"Dakota Walker. Carter is my brother. He doesn't talk much." He explains, looking to his brother who still hasn't said a word.

"What do you think, Grease?" I ask my VP after a few moments.

"First thing they need to do is get their asses in there and start cleaning shit up." Grease growls, they both jump up and head into the shop to start cleaning up.

"When they finish, give them a ride home." I comment as the two of us watch them from my office door.

"I'll make sure they get there." He murmurs.

"Good. I'm going back home. I'll see you tomorrow." I slap him on the back as I head out.

Chapter 6
Jade

Reaper and I met with his lawyer this morning to go over what we would need to do in order for us to take over responsibility for Cole.

According to him it should be fairly easy to do since he is a child that was born during their marriage although he is not biologically Reaper's son.

He promised to contact Brandi's lawyer to get all the paperwork ready for signing as soon as possible since Brandi wanted to be gone by next week.

I'm currently headed to the clubhouse that is located on the back side of Reaper's property behind the main house. The property sits on a corner of two different roads so technically you don't have to drive past the main house to get to it. Since it is within walking distance I had rather park my car at the house and walk over leaving the lot open for other vehicles.

The entire club is having a cookout tonight. All the brothers and their old ladies will be there with their kids. The single guys may bring someone but they know to be on their best behavior. Thank goodness the club has changed a lot since Reaper's dad, Ace, was the President.

Back then, it was a lot more wild and a lot more illegal. There are no actual club hang arounds here that willingly share themselves with all the brothers. These days, the hang arounds are friends. Sometimes the brothers may date one, see if it's a relationship that can go the distance and sometimes it does. But there are still some girls that try to sleep their way through all the guys.

Bones and his wife Joanne, they met during a bar-b-que several years ago when she was invited by Fire one weekend.

Everyone thought Bones would be single forever until he met Joanne. They are both the oldest in our group. It surprised everyone when Bones, so grumpy, took a shine to sweet little Joanne. They were simply made for each other. I left before they got married though, so missed that.

I walk into the clubhouse a little while later and see Maria, Chucky's old lady, handing out cookies to the kids. Amber finally notices me after shoving the whole thing in her mouth.

"Mommy!" she runs towards me, wrapping herself around my legs.

"Hey Munchkin! You aren't filling up on sweets are you?" I smile down at her as she shakes her head, stuffing yet another cookie into her mouth.

"Hope I didn't overstep by giving her the cookies." Maria says with a smile.

—

"Not at all. But she will try to sneak them so watch her like a hawk!" I tickle Amber on the stomach as she goes to run with the other kids.

"She's an absolute doll. We are just getting the meat ready for the guys while they get the grill going." She says as we walk into the kitchen.

"Hey, where have you been all day?" Fire demands from the counter.

"Reaper and I had to meet with his lawyer earlier." I don't mention anything about Cole as nothing is set in stone yet.

"I know he'll be glad to be rid of that bitch." Maria grumbles. I couldn't believe everything he's had to go through with her when Chucky explained it all to me. Poor boy."

"He tell you about the time I set the cabin on fire with him inside?" Fire asks, catching Maria's attention.

My mind drifts off thinking about what all he has had to go through with Brandi all these years. I also think about how I wasn't here to help him through it. But I'm here now and I'm not going anywhere.

Reaper

It's been a good night just hanging out with the club family. Amber is currently asleep in my lap where she crawled into it about an hour ago.

"Want me to go find somewhere to lay her down?" Jade whispers to me.

"Nah, let's just go ahead and head home. Most of these guys will stay here all night anyway." I answer, standing up with Amber in my arms.

We say our goodnights to those we pass and walk to the house. I place Amber in her room that I had fixed up for her. Most of the colors in this room are a light shade of purple which she picked out. Jade thought I had lost my mind allowing a three year old to pick the color but it worked out just fine.

Tucking her in, I kiss her head and go in search of her mother. I find her in the master bedroom pulling clothes out of an overnight bag she must have dropped off before coming over to the clubhouse.

"I'm going to get a shower before we lay down. I smell like smoke from the fire." She looks up at me expectantly.

"I'll join you." I stalk towards her, grabbing her to me as she wraps her legs around my waist.

I walk us both into the master bath, setting her on the counter. I turn away for a moment to start the shower up before turning back to her.

Taking my time, I slowly pull her shirt up over her head, tossing it on the floor. Her breasts are still covered by her bra which I get rid of quickly and watch as her nipples are revealed to my eyes.

I slowly look away from her eyes as I feast on her perfect globes in front of me.

I blow my hot breath on her and watch in amazement as her nipple peaks up even more begging me to pull it into my mouth.

Slowly I lick her pointy peaks with the tip of my tongue causing her to sigh and press her breasts out even further towards me.

I don't need more of an invitation than that as I pull her breast into my mouth, swirling my tongue around the nipple. Letting it go with a pop, I quickly pull the other into my mouth giving it the same attention.

I'm already hard as a rock inside my pants just from listening to her moans. Looking up I see her eyes glazed over with desire. Standing her up, I quickly pull the rest of her clothes off revealing her beautiful body to me.

Unable to resist, I sit her back on the counter and spread her legs wide as I kneel down between her thighs.

She smells so sweet it makes my mouth water. I don't take time to let her know what is coming before I dive my tongue deep within her slick slit.

Pretty soon she's coming hard as her insides try to clamp down on my tongue that is fucking her quickly. I lick her through it until she calms again.

Standing up, I strip off all of my own clothes as I watch her breathing hard after my onslaught.

Picking her up, she wraps those beautiful legs around me as I step into the shower still holding her.

Pressing her back into the shower wall, I grind my hard cock into her slick wet heat, kissing her deeply.

"I need you now, Jade." I whisper, rubbing back and forth with my tip just waiting for her to give the go ahead before I slam home where I am always supposed to be.

She shakes her head at me but I need more than that from her.

"Words baby, I need your words." I groan as my tip once again strokes her folds.

"Yes, Rafe. Please." She finally begs.

Pulling back, I slam home in one stroke, fitting easily within her wet heat. I can't stop the groan I let out at the feeling of her surrounding my cock, squeezing tightly.

—

At first I slowly pull out then thrust in again but it doesn't take long before my pace builds up quickly. I don't slam into her as hard as I would like, afraid that I will hurt her but soon she has something to say about it.

"Harder, Rafe." she growls, clawing my back.

Getting a tighter grip on her ass, I slam in as hard as I can. The feeling is amazing and apparently she loves it as well if her moans are any indication.

I lower my head, sucking one of her nipples into my mouth and start to bite it a little. That seems to do the trick, as I feel her pussy clamp down on my cock.

Screaming out her release, she pushes me over the edge. I let my balls empty everything they have deep inside of her.

It is only at this moment that I realize that I forgot a condom. Not that I would mind another baby with her but I want to be sure it is what she wants as well before we go down that road again.

"Fuck baby, I'm sorry." I whisper, lowering her to her own feet.

"For what?" She asks with confusion.

"I forgot to put on a condom." I whisper, truly sorry to put her in this position yet again.

"It's okay Rafe. I trust you. Plus I'm on the pill, so everything should be fine." She explains with a smile, easing the tension that I could feel at the thought of losing her again because of my own stupidity.

We finish our shower, each washing the other, taking our time. We don't get out until the water has long since turned cold.

Tucking her in next to me in my bed, I hold her tightly afraid that I'll wake in the morning and she'll be gone again.

I drift off to sleep shortly after she does.

Jade

I wake the next morning to the sounds of laughter and the smell of food. Following both to the kitchen, I find Reaper standing next to Amber who is standing on a chair at the counter. Apparently he is helping her to make pancakes on a griddle.

"Look mommy, I'm cooking for you!" She says excitedly as I walk further into the room.

"Oh, it smells so good! You are doing an amazing job lovebug." I smile watching as she pours more batter, half of which lands on the counter instead of the griddle.

"Okay, that's enough pancakes. Why don't you go sit at the table with mommy and I'll bring them over?" Reaper says to Amber.

She quickly hops down, grabs my hand and pulls me towards the table. Reaper walks over with the pile of pancakes and takes the seat next to my own.

Leaning over, he kisses me softly.

"Good morning, beautiful." He murmurs with a smile before turning to the pile of food and putting one on Amber's plate. I help her to pour the syrup so that she doesn't get it everywhere.

We are just finishing up breakfast when Reaper's phone rings. It must be MC business as he takes it outside on the porch. While all of their businesses are legal, they still skirt the law depending on the situation. Therefore they still keep things between the men and leave the women mostly in the dark.

"I need to go to the shop for just a bit. Do you have any plans for today?" He asks a few minutes later when he comes back inside.

"I'm supposed to meet Maria, Joanna and Fire at Clyde's in a little while. They are wanting to discuss the plans for the benefit carnival in town this year." I answer.

"Yeah, that's coming up next month. Just make sure Joanna puts one of the other brothers in the dunk tank this time. All the other guys lined up to dunk me last year, it's time for a little bit of payback." He grumbles as if put out last year.

I laugh, wishing I had been here to see it. I probably would have dunked him myself.

After saying goodbye to both myself and Amber, he heads out. I get myself and Amber ready to go, send Fire a text that I will meet them there.

Reaper

Arriving at the shop, I walk in and find several of the brothers busy with other projects. While we do a lot of log trailers, sometimes we get other stuff that needs a quick welding fix from the regular public.

"What was so important, Grease?" I demand, walking into the office.

That's when I notice the two boys that Grease had caught breaking into our shop sitting on the couch. Wondering what they could have done now, I wait for my VP to explain.

"I found these two in the back lot sleeping in one of the old broken down trucks." Grease says, crossing his arms.

"Where were they sleeping in the truck?" I ask, not fully understanding.

"I have no fucking clue and neither one of them will give an answer. Thought I'd let you take a shot at it." He growls, looking at Carter and Dakota.

"I would suggest the two of you give an answer before we just call the sheriff out here to deal with the two of you." I glare at the boys.

"We don't have anywhere to go." Dakota says with a sigh.

"What do you mean? Don't you have family? Surely the two of you still live at home with your parents." I look at the two of them and realize they are both dirty as if they haven't had a shower in weeks.

Come to think of it, they looked the same the night they were caught breaking in. At the time, I just thought it was from messing up my shop.

"No family. We were in the boys home until we aged out but there was nowhere for us to go besides the homeless shelter. I swore years ago we would never be in another one." Dakota explains further.

"Both of you aged out, so the two of you are twins?" I ask.

"Yes sir." Dakota answers. So the two are twins but not identical as they are so very different in both looks and personalities.

"I can talk to you outside a minute Prez?" Grease finally says in the silence.

"You two stay right there. We will be back in a few minutes." I say to the boys as I follow Grease out into the main part of the shop.

"Calling the cops won't help anything. They would just drop the two of them at the closest homeless shelter and they would both just run away from it. They seem scared of the place." Grease says.

"Yeah, I got that feeling from them as well. I just don't know what we should do with them. We certainly can't let them keep sleeping in the junk pile. It's too dangerous for them to be back there." I run my hand over my face trying to think of a solution.

"What about Bones? Him and his wife may take them in. I know Joanna would anyway." Grease volunteers.

"We would have to talk to her and let her talk to Bones. He's a grump and only she can get away with shit." I laugh at the thought.

"That's true. If left to Bones he'd probably just say no and walk away. We should get Joanna down here first." Grease says.

"Joanna and the other girls are meeting in town to go over the plans for the carnival next month. Let's give them time to finish up and I will text her to come by the shop. For now, put the boys to work. Have them sweep the floors or something." Grease goes back into the office to put the boys to work.

I go grab my welding gear and put in a few hours of hard labor myself.

"Reaper said he absolutely was not doing the dunk tank this year." At my admission, Joanna laughs uncontrollably.

"Remind me to find the video from last year so you can see it. It was epic!" She says, wiping a tear from her eye.

"Reaper didn't tell me there was a video!" I exclaim with excitement.

"He's probably hoping we all have forgotten about it." Maria smiles.

"I wasn't planning to have just one of the guys in the dunk tank this year. I plan to split the days in half so that each one gets time in it. I want a video of them all being dunked so we can play it over and over again as we laugh at their asses!" Joanna states.

We all laugh at the thought of being able to see everyone get dunked. It'll be a video we can use against them for years to come.

Joanna's phone pings with a text that she reads silently.

"I need to go ladies. We'll get together again next week to discuss anything that isn't going to plan." She says as she stands up to leave.

"I wonder what that was about?" Fire asks, watching Joanna through the window as she gets in her car to leave.

"If it's important, she'll tell us soon enough." Maria murmurs.

"So how are you liking your job?" Fire asks me.

"It's okay. It's not really what I wanted to do." I shrug my shoulders.

"What do you want to do?" Maria asks with interest.

"I was in school back in New Orleans to be a kindergarten teacher." I answer.

"Yes, but is that what you really want to do? People go to school for all kinds of things. It's not necessarily their passion." Maria states.

Her question throws me off guard for a moment. I've never really thought about what my passion is. It's definitely something to think about.

"Well, I need to run." Fire says as she stands up.

"Yeah, I do as well. I need to run by the grocery store before heading home." Maria stands up as well.

We all say our goodbyes. I only stay a little bit longer to give Amber time to finish her ice cream she ordered when we first got here.

As we are getting into my car, my phone pings with a text from Mrs. Morris. I quickly head towards the daycare center.

Reaper

"You wanted to see me?" Joanna asks as she comes through my office door.

"Yeah, I have a question for you. Come have a seat." I motion her forward.

"Everything is okay isn't it? I was afraid something had happened to one of you." She sighs with relief after looking around.

"I'm sorry. We are all fine as you can see. There are two new faces out there today though." I comment.

"Yes, I saw the two young men sweeping the floor. They can't be no more than eighteen or nineteen. Are they new prospects?" She asks, still confused as to why she is here.

"Not exactly. That may be an option we can give them at a later time. I was wanting to see if you would be willing to take them in? They are basically homeless. Grease found the two sleeping in the junk pile on the back side of the property. Apparently they were in the group home until they aged out but they had nowhere to go. They both seem scared of the homeless shelter." I explain.

"I'm sure they have a good reason. There's all kinds of crazies in those places. I wouldn't be surprised what they have seen if they were ever in one." Joanna, having grown up hard, knows what it is like to be homeless.

Her mother went from one shelter to the other when Joanna was really young until her grandmother took her in after her mom's death.

Since she went through all of that, Joanna decided two years ago that she wanted to open a house for mothers who were homeless with kids.

She's been working with contractors for over a year to design the perfect house for such a project. The club donated the ten acres it will sit on which is right up against the clubhouse property.

"Does Bones know about this plan?" She asks with a half smile.

"I haven't said anything to him yet. Grease and I thought it best to leave that part to you." At my admission, she laughs out loud.

"I'll take care of it. Can you call the boys in here for a minute so that I can talk to them?" She asks.

I walk out into the shop and send the two in the office to talk with Joanna. A few minutes later they all three walk out smiling. Even Dakota who is more quiet than his brother.

Jade

When I get to the daycare, Amber runs ahead with me trailing behind. By the time I walk in, she is already on the other side of the room playing with Cole.

"What happened?" I ask Mrs. Morris.

"Brandi never showed up yesterday afternoon to pick him up and we have been unable to reach her by phone. Last time she showed up the next morning so that's why I waited before calling anyone." Mrs. Morris explains.

"She's done this before?" I'm floored at the thought of a mother not remembering her child.

"Several times actually." Mrs. Morris sighs.

"Did you call children services?" I ask.

"No. I only texted you. Mr. Star is actually listed as the second emergency contact on Cole's file. Brandi told one of my workers last week that you two would be taking Cole in soon. So, that's why I got in touch with you first." She wrings her hands as if not sure what she should have done.

"I appreciate you texting me. Reaper and I will take care of it. We're actually looking at taking him from Brandi but she can't just leave him. Our lawyers will need her to sign the papers on Monday." I explain, worried about where she has run off to and if this is just another stunt to not have to sign the divorce papers.

"Well everything he has is in his backpack. There's no extra clothes but there is a jacket." She shrugs one shoulder helplessly.

"It'll be fine Mrs. Morris, thank you." I squeeze her shoulder, walking over to the kids.

"Amber, you want to introduce me to your friend?" I say, kneeling down to be eye level with the two.

"Dis is Cole, mommy." She says in her sweet little voice.

"Would you and Cole like to go shopping for a little while? Get some new clothes?" I ask, looking over the rags he is currently wearing.

His shirt and jeans are really old, dirty and torn as well as his shoes.

At my question, two little pairs of eyes look up at me. It's got to be a good sign that he is willing to acknowledge my presence.

Holding out my hands, they each grab one as we all stand up, heading out the door. Getting the pair into the car, I realize the first thing I need to buy is another booster seat. No worries, I think to myself, we'll get everything he needs before we head back to Reaper's house. Then I need to tell him what is going on and see if we can find Brandi.

Several hours later we finished at the clothing store. Cole never really commented on anything that was picked out for him. A few times I caught him smiling at a few things and Amber seemed to answer for him. It was cute watching the two of them together.

We arrived at the shoe store a few minutes ago. Amber is currently clutching a pair of little pink sandals she spotted as soon as we walked in.

I try to wait to see if anything really catches Cole's eye instead of suggesting anything to him. I'm absolutely sure the sweet boy understands way more than others have given him credit for.

Watching silently, I notice he keeps going back to the same little pair of boots that look similar to the ones that Reaper wears all the time.

Kneeling down, I pick them up looking at them.

"You like these?" I ask him directly. I wasn't really expecting him to answer but I gasp in surprise when he speaks.

"Yes ma'am." He whispers shyly at me. I smile as I find the correct size for him to try on.

"Let's see how they look." I reach down and help him to change out of his old shoes.

Once the new ones are on his feet, I check to be sure there is room in the toe for him to still grow into them a little bit.

"I really like those. Are these the ones you want?" I ask, waiting to see if he will speak again.

Instead he just shakes his head with a huge smile and I take that as a yes. Taking our purchases to the front, I quickly pay the clerk and leave the store with two very happy little kids.

I can't stop the smile on my face as I point the car towards the house. Despite how it all started, today was a great day. Now, to talk to Reaper.

Reaper

I'm just finishing up at the shop when I get a text from Jade asking when I will be getting home from work. I text her back to let her know I will be there shortly.

"Prez." I hear growled from my office door. Looking up I see Bones who looks like he ate something sour.

"Bones." I acknowledge with a smile, waiting to see what he says since I know exactly why he is at my office door.

"Mind telling me why I now have two homeless hellions living in my house?" He asks, plopping down in the chair in front of my desk.

"Because your wife is an amazing woman?" I ask back, trying not to chuckle at his expression.

Bones has always had a sour disposition. Only his wife is able to see the softer side of him and also the only one that can push him into doing something he doesn't really want to do.

"I know it was your idea." He grumbles, crossing his arms. At that point, I do start laughing.

"Come on, man. It's not that bad." I say when I am able to control myself.

"You don't get it, Reaper." He rubs his face with exasperation.

"I didn't know it would bother you this much, man. The boys needed help and Joanna was the only one I could think of." I explain, still not fully understanding his problem with giving Carter and Dakota a place to stay.

"She'll get attached to them!" He exclaims, eyes bugging out.

I think I'm starting to understand now, as I lean back in my chair.

"And you think that's a bad thing?" I sigh.

"What if she gets attached and they leave? We weren't able to have our own kids but she'll get to where she sees them as hers. What if they leave?" He asks.

"What if they get attached to Joanna and you? Have you thought about that?" I counter.

He sits back, stunned as if he never thought about that at all. I smile at him again, knowing full well he is also afraid of getting attached to them as well.

Him and Joanna wanted to adopt after they got married but it never happened for them. One day, the adoption agency finally told them they were actually considered to be too old to adopt a child. It devastated them both.

"Hey, Prez? You and Bones gotta see this." Looking to the door, we both see Loki standing there.

We walk over as he nods his head at something across the shop. Looking in that direction, we can see Dakota putting together a small engine that was needing to be rebuilt.

___

90

I'm not sure if the boy knows what he is doing so we start walking in that direction. Not saying a word, we watch over his shoulder as he continues working on it.

We can clearly see he knows exactly what he is doing and never looks up in our direction.

"He's dismantled and put together lawn mower engines plus others since we were in grade school." His brother Carter says, stepping up next to us.

"He's fucking fast." Bones grunts in awe from my other side and I agree with him.

I've never seen anyone put one together so quickly before. The boy must be some type of genius or something.

"Let me know when he gets it back together and on the bike. I want to know if it all works correctly. I'm heading home." I slap Bones on the shoulder as I leave them all still watching Dakota work.

Jade

I'm in the kitchen cooking spaghetti when I hear the roar of Reaper's bike pulling up in the driveway.

Maria walked over from the clubhouse when I got home earlier. After helping me to unload the car, I explained to her what happened and why I now had Cole with me.

She took both the kids with her over to the clubhouse to give me time to explain everything to Reaper. I wasn't exactly sure what his reaction would be. I knew he'd be pissed that Brandi had just left Cole without a word though to anyone.

"Babe?" I heard him from the front door as he walked in.

"In the kitchen!" I answer as I stir the sauce in the pan.

Walking in, he comes straight to me, leaning down for a kiss.

"This smells so good. Where's Amber?" He asks, picking up a spoon to taste the sauce.

"She's with Maria at the moment. I need to talk to you for a minute." I say, looking at him.

"This is already not sounding good." He grumbles, looking back at me.

"Cole is here." I say in a rush.

"What? Why?" He asks, confused.

"Mrs. Morris from the daycare called me. Brandi never picked him up yesterday afternoon. She's tried calling her several times without any luck. So she called me instead. I went to get him after leaving the restaurant." I explain.

"She actually left him without a damn word? That fucking bitch is a horrible ass excuse for a mother! Fuck!" He growls, slamming his hands down on the counter. "She better not have run off before signing those fucking papers. I'll kill her ass this time!"

I believe deep down that he really would like to but she is a woman. None of the guys would willingly hurt a woman, even if she really deserved it. I couldn't swear on that when it came to the women in the club. My sister would slit a throat in a heartbeat if she believed they needed to die.

While the MC owns mostly legal businesses, the guys were all from the backwoods and believed in backwoods justice when needed.

"I'll go call our lawyer. I have his home number and see what he says. Then I need to call the guys in. We have to find her. Not just for the divorce. That little boy deserves better." He says gruffly, kissing me on the head before leaving the room.

Chapter 8
Reaper

After finding out that Brandi ran off again and this time leaving Cole without a word to anyone, I put a call in to Skeeter down in New Orleans. He's the President of our sister chapter down there and has one of the best computer tech guys in the club. If there is any type of trail at all, Buzz would be the one to find it.

I've held off on bringing the situation to the club during Church. Not yet knowing what we are dealing with, I'm not really sure what to tell the guys anyway.

Jade has taken the role of mother to both the kids with a smile on her face. Cole is a great kid. He doesn't talk much but, I can tell he's taking everything in. Constantly watching what is going on around him.

Walking into the shop, I go in search of Chucky. He's supposed to be making a run later in the week to pick up our shipment coming in from Texas.

This will be our last shipment signaling the end to our illegal operations. The money the club has been saving up will go into opening up several more bars in our area and possibly a strip club up in Memphis. There's always money to be made when whiskey and pussy is involved.

"Hey, Prez, you got a package early this morning. I put it on your desk." Loki says as I walk by.

Not even looking in his direction, I head straight into the office. I plop down into my office chair and as I do so, a loud air horn nearly blows out my ear drum making me jump out of my chair.

Loki is laughing his fool head off from the door.

"You little mother fucker, get your ass back to work. Your pranks are going to get your head bashed in." I growl in his direction.

"Sorry, Prez, it was meant for Grease but his ass never would sit down earlier and I forgot about it being there." Loki pleads from the door.

"Because I knew it was there. Figured I would let you piss off the Prez enough for him to beat you to death with your own arms." Grease calmly explains walking into the office with a smile.

"Will any of you fucks ever grow the hell up?" I ask, holding my head in my hand with a sign.

"Hell no! Like I tell Maria, she's the only grown up in our relationship." Chucky adds, walking in to take a seat on the couch across the office.

"Don't you all have work to do?" I ask, picking up the package that is on my desk.

"It's break time." Grease says, taking out a sandwich from a bag he got out of the fridge.

Shaking my head, I open the package. At first I am not sure what I am looking at but, it all sinks in as I look at a picture that was included.

"Motherfucker!" I grit out through clenched teeth.

"What is it?" Grease asks, coming to look over my shoulder, his lunch forgotten for the moment.

"Bones!!" I yell through the door and wait for him to come in. "Get Joanna to drive over to the house. Tell her to get Jade and the kids to the clubhouse and keep them within sight." He doesn't ask why, just leaves to do my bidding.

"The rest of you, get everyone to the clubhouse. We go on lock down in two hours." No one says a word, just leaves to do as asked. They know I would never demand a lock down unless it was absolutely necessary.

As everyone leaves, I pick up my phone trying to call Jade. She doesn't answer so I send a quick text instead before climbing on my bike and heading to the clubhouse myself.

Jade

The first thing I feel before opening my eyes is the pain in the back of my head. The last thing I remember is walking out onto the porch to call the kids in for a snack.

Something hard hit the back of my head as I walked out the door and everything went black. It takes a minute for my eyes to adjust to the dark room.

I have no idea where I am, there's no window to see out of. I'm unsure what time it is or how long I have been here. I begin to worry about the kids, hoping that whoever did this didn't get a hold of Amber and Cole too.

"My poor babies." I whisper into the dark as tears begin to stream from my eyes.

I think I hear voices from far away and strain my ears to try to understand what is being said.

A scream sounds from somewhere that sends a chill down my back.

A few minutes later I can hear someone unlocking my door and I back up against the wall behind me.

I'm blinded by a bright flashlight as the door opens. Whoever it is doesn't say a word as I hear them set something down before leaving again.

A minute later, the room I'm in floods with light. There's a small table near the door with a plate of food. I guess this is what they brought in, keeping the light off so that I couldn't see their faces.

Running over to the door, I begin banging my fists.

"Let me out! What do you want with me?" I scream out in frustration but get no reply.

Feeling defeated, I sit down on the cot I was on when I woke up. I'm so thirsty but afraid to eat or drink what they left for me. They could have it laced with something.

Curling myself up, I weep silently as I pray that Reaper can find me. I also pray as hard as I can that the children are safe at the clubhouse and not in this hell hole somewhere.

Reaper

Pulling up to the clubhouse, I'm not even completely off my bike when Bones, Joanna and Grease run up to me.

"I couldn't find Jade." Joanna says frantically.

"What do you mean you couldn't find her?" I growl.

Joanna shrinks back from the tone in my voice and I'm immediately sorry for talking to her that way.

"I went to the house myself, Jade and the kids are not there. The front door was wide open and there were snacks on the table as if they were getting ready to eat." Bones says, holding Joanna under his arm.

"So they've been taken?" I groan as I feel a pit open deep inside.

"We don't know that for sure. We need to get everyone inside then call Church. You need to let everyone in on what has happened so far. If they've been taken, we will get them back!" Grease says with a steady voice.

I nod my head and watch as they move away to help everyone get settled inside.

Letting my anger settle within me, a calmness finally washes over me. They don't call me the Reaper for nothing.

I can control my anger like a weapon. Only letting it out when I get ready to do so.

Whoever is on the receiving end of it will get no mercy from me.

We all file into our meeting room, no one saying a word until the door is closed and locked.

"What's going on, Prez?" Loki asks from the end of the table.

"The Abyss have decided to try to start a war. The package I received earlier today was their demand for us to clear out of Memphis completely." I say to my men.

"They think because we've gone legit that we will just roll over then. " Grease adds and I nod my head.

All the guys start talking at once, banging my hand on the table and I quiet them down.

"That's not all. They sent a picture." Taking it out of my vest pocket I throw it on the table for them all to see.

"Oh, fuck. Who is it?" Loki asks, picking it up.

"It's Brandi. I recognize the bracelet. At this point we can assume they have Jade and the kids. The note on the back is a threat to do the same to her."

All the guys sit quietly for a minute until there is a banging on the door. I know exactly who it is because only she would be stupid enough to interrupt a Church meeting. Instead of answering, I ignore the banging.

"We need to find out where these assholes have been staying for the last year and if they have any warehouses we don't know about. We have to find my girl and my kids before they do something to them." I growl out to the men over the banging that is getting louder.

"How long do we have?" Grease asks loudly.

"They said they would be in touch by tomorrow." I roll my eyes as the banging begins to beat out a song tempo.

Having had enough of it, I get up and jerk the door open.

"About damn time you fucker!" Fire glares at me.

"You know damn well you are not supposed to interrupt! We don't have time for your fucking drama!" I scream at her.

"Too fucking bad you giant ape fuck! The kids are in the kitchen. I found them hiding in the woods." Her news instantly relaxes me just a little.

"Oh thank fuck! Are they hurt?" I ask about to check for myself.

"They are both fine. I just thought you'd want to know they were here. Amber said they were playing and went back to the house. She couldn't find her mommy, so they were trying to walk down here." Fire says.

"So neither of them saw anything?" I sigh.

"No. I didn't tell them anything either. They are too young to understand it. Maria has them in the kitchen making cookies." Fire looks at me with regret for not having anything more for me to go on.

"Thank you." I say before closing the door back again.

"Thank God the kids are okay. That's two less worries." Chucky rubs his head as if trying to stop his head from hurting.

"I'll call Skeeter down in New Orleans, give them an update on the information we have. I called them this morning about finding Brandi because I thought she just ran off and left Cole behind as a way to not have to sign the divorce papers. Guess I should have given her the benefit of the doubt." I shake my head, unable to look at the picture again.

"You think Brandi is still alive?" Loki asks.

"No. Or if she is, she soon won't be. They would have used her to get information on the club and Jade. Once they had it, they would have no use for her." I sigh feeling bad for what I am sure has happened to a woman I thought I once loved.

"The rest of you put in calls to all your contacts in Memphis. We need to find Jade.

NOW!" I growl, pushing my chair away before walking out the door to check on the kids.

Jade

The lights in the room were shut off again at some point. It must have pissed someone off that I refused to eat or drink what they brought in for me. When the lights came on again, there was a note sitting next to a fresh glass of water and the same food as before.

EAT OR WE FORCE YOU

Picking up the sandwich, I smell of it first and my mouth begins to water so I take a small bite. Before I know it, I've eaten the whole sandwich and swallowed every sip of water in the cup.

I still don't know how long I have been in this room but it was long enough for the bread on the sandwich to have dried out a little.

Whoever was doing all the screaming stopped doing so at least several hours ago. I'm fairly sure they don't have the kids, whoever these people are.

I'm almost certain this has something to do with the club. While I know they have tried to go completely legal because the club didn't want any more of the brothers serving prison time for gun running or drugs, the club has been around long enough to have plenty of enemies.

Everyone around knows that someone killed Reaper's parents by cutting a brake line even though it could never be proven. Reaper nor any of the other club members would ever say who they believed did it. Knowing Reaper, he probably knows exactly who it was and has been biding his time to get the revenge that he feels is justified in his soul. The same holds true for the rest of the guys.

I'm not naive about what they are capable of doing. Honestly, I would think that I would be capable of the same when it comes to those important to me.

Especially my children. In my heart they are both mine. Cole became mine the very second he took my hand the day I picked him up from Mrs. Morris' daycare center.

I don't believe that he is on the spectrum though. He actually doesn't seem to be any different at all, just quiet. As if he's learned that is what he's supposed to do. Be quiet. And with having a mother like Brandi, it probably was a learned behavior. One I intend to break.

He needs to be a kid. I plan on making sure that happens for him. As soon as I can get the hell out of here.

Chapter 9
Reaper

Skeeter showed up at the club house an hour ago. I'm antsy and ready to move. It's been hours since she was taken from my own fucking house. The bastards.

Buzz didn't come with Skeeter, he stayed behind to use his own computer systems but has been sending us updated information all afternoon.

One of Chucky's contacts called to let us know about an old warehouse that he's seen the Abyss coming and going from over the last week.

Area photos that Buzz was able to get show that they are definitely using the place in some capacity.

The only problem is that it's in an area that's hard to get into without being seen. With our clubhouse being two and half hours away, it's hard to move so many guys at once without them knowing that we are coming.

"What if we load everyone up in a van trailer pulled by a Peterbilt?" Chucky finally speaks up after we've all gone over plan after plan that would never work.

"That could totally fucking work." Grease sits up at the comment.

"Our big truck has our business name on the side of it though." I say.

"We'll borrow one of the ones sitting around the yard. It's a warehousing district so they would never look twice at a big truck coming through." Chucky explains further.

"He has a point. Looking at the aerials, the warehouses around it all get traffic all day every day. So another big truck coming in wouldn't cause an alarm." Buzz says from the speaker phone.

"Okay, then let's make this work. Where do we unload the guys?" I ask.

"Let me call Brian O'Neil. I'm sure he knows someone around there that owns one of the warehouses. He could get us access in an area we could unload and sneak over to the area they are located." Grease says, raising his phone to his ear at the nod of my head.

"Chucky, go get the truck and trailer. Everyone else strap up and be ready to load up as soon as he gets back. I want to be on the road in no more than a fucking hour." I demand.

Jade

I must have dozed off for a while even though I tried to stay awake. I was right that the food was laced with something. As I wake up, I realize that my eyes are covered with some type of cloth and I am tied to a chair.

I hear something from across the room and turn my head in that direction.

"Ah, finally awake I see." I hear a deep voice that is closer to me now. "So beautiful." He whispers making me jump as I feel his fingers touching the side of my breast.

"What do you want from me?" My voice cracks but I hold off the tears, truly afraid of what these guys might do to me.

"You are my leverage to keep that fucker away from Memphis. As long as you play nice, we'll let you go when we are done." He whispers again, stroking my cheek before I hear him walking away.

I could tell from his voice that the only way they will be letting me go, is after I am dead or worse, used by them all.

I try to loosen the ropes tying my hands to the sides of the chair but it refuses to give an inch.

"I'd suggest you be still." The deep voice says from somewhere across the room.

I hear a door open then footsteps coming closer.

"No one has left the Night Howler's clubhouse although a few bikes did ride in. Looks like they called in the chapter from further South." The newest guy says.

"I expected that. Just as I expect he'll come for her regardless of my little present I sent to him." Deep voice chuckles.

"I can't wait to play with this little piece. I wonder if she's a screamer like the other bitch." The new voice says, coming closer until I can feel him breathing on my face.

Out of nowhere I feel his tongue lick up the side of my throat and I rear back spitting in what I hope is his face.

"Mmm, I love a fighter." I can hear the smile in his voice and I shiver at the thought of him touching me again.

"Go make sure the guys are ready." Deep voice demands.

"I just told you that they haven't even left their clubhouse." The creep whines a little.

"Reaper is smart! He'll figure out a way to get out of there without any of us knowing. He'll know we are watching. So go make sure the other fucks are ready!" Deep voice demands again and I listen as the creep walks away, slamming the door behind him.

"Why are you doing this?" I ask.

"Reaper took something from me that should have been mine when his old man died."

Deep voice says after contemplating the question for several minutes.

"What did he take?" I ask curiously.

"Control." He says simply.

"Control? Control of what? The MC was always supposed to be his." I state.

"He didn't want it though. Not the way it was. If he did, the club would still be making bank with guns and drugs! But NO! He wanted the club to go legit but he didn't stop there. He also stopped anyone else from running in Night Howler's territory. Fucking Axe was supposed to die without naming a successor. Instead, he left a letter behind in case anything happened to him and I had to leave before anyone found out I was involved!"

"Grant?" I ask quietly.

"No one has called me that in a really long time. I'm surprised you even remember my name." He says quietly to me.

"You were Axe's best friend. How could you?" I ask accusingly.

"That mother fucker was going soft! Everyone could see it. I had to try to make sure the club stayed true. Instead his softass son took over and made a mockery of what we stood for!" He screams at me.

"Axe knew guns were only killing kids. He knew as well as everyone else that it was time for a change. You should be ashamed of yourself!" I scream back just before I feel a hard slap across my face.

"You stupid little bitch! Don't talk to me that way or I'll let Bang come back in here and do as he pleases." He growls at me.

He hit me so hard it knocked the cloth off of my head and I can see him clearly now. I don't remember him from all those years ago. I was only a kid. He's older now though, going gray at the temples. He's wearing a vest that says Abyss MC on the back with flames coming off of it.

He turns around and notices the cloth is gone from my eyes but doesn't move to put it back. He just curls his lip in my direction as he heads out of the door.

I pray that Reaper stays safe. Grant was right about one thing, Reaper would come from me but he was wrong about Reaper being soft.

I never tried to listen much to the stories that were always circling around. They were just stories right? But right now I am thinking there may be a truth in those stories that I didn't want to really acknowledge.

Do I care at the moment that the man I love might possibly kill in order to save me? Hell no. Just as long as he washes that shit off before coming through the house on my clean floors. He gets that shit in the carpet and I'll kill him myself. I smile to myself. I must be going crazy or turning into my sister. I frown at the thought.

Reaper

"Thank fuck Chucky got a temperature controlled trailer, otherwise we'd all be dead from the heat." Bud says from his position against the wall.

Bud is one of the more serious guys in the club. He got his name from his favorite drink. Most people think it's short for Buddy but it's not. Even as a teenager you rarely saw him without a beer can in his hand.

The nickname stuck after a party we had back in high school when he drank everyone under the table and was still going strong after everyone else passed out. He even managed to pick the rest of us up out of the yard, getting us into the house so that we didn't freeze to death.

"It's supposed to be in the hundreds next week. Hope the air in the garage doesn't go out again like it did last year. We couldn't get you guys to get shit done without complaining." Grease says.

"The Devil shouldn't have been trying to burn us all alive." Loki comments.

"Better than you burning us all alive like you almost did several months back." Aero throws into the conversation getting a laugh out of Loki.

"I heard about that. Skeeter here would have skinned your ass alive for that one." Mick,

Road Captain of the New Orleans chapter comments.

"It wasn't that big of a bomb." Loki laughs.

"It was big enough that we had to replace the fucking bathroom in the shop!" Grease growls.

"You guys seriously can't take a joke." Loki shakes his head.

"You know what Loki? I seriously hope that one day you have a house full of little shits just like you. And when you do, I'll be right there to help them make your life hell." Grease smiles broadly as Loki's face falls at the thought.

"I'm not having kids. Stuck with one woman forever? No thanks man. Besides, these Mississippi women are nuts. Just look at Fire for instance." Loki's words have everyone looking to Spark for his reaction in which all he does is groan.

"Fuck, he's right. They are bat shit fucking crazy." Spark says as everyone laughs.

"Shit, man, that's all women no matter where they are from. You just have to pick the crazy that's right for you and hang on to her." Skeeter has everyone laughing at that.

It's good to let the guys joke around with what we are about to walk into. We never know what could happen or if all of us will make it back in one piece.

Chapter 10
Jade

I've been alone in this room since Grant walked out over an hour ago. I really need to go pee but I try not to think about it as I constantly work to loosen the knots on the rope. I can feel it giving just a little at a time.

My wrists are extremely sore and bleeding from trying so hard. A few more tugs and my right arm is free. Not taking the time to examine my wrist, I quickly untie myself completely.

My legs almost give out on me as I put my weight on them after being in the chair for so long. Righting myself, I make my way over to the door and peer out.

Not seeing anyone, I start to make a run for it but don't get far when I am grabbed by the hair at the back of my head causing me to scream out.

"Where the fuck do you think you are going?" Bang snarls into my face.

Not answering him, I watch as he looks around as if to see if the coast is clear then he looks back at me with a grin.

"Time for some fun." He jerks me to him as he rubs himself into me.

I begin to try to fight him off, clawing at his face that he pushes into my neck and he jerks back slapping me hard.

"I do so love a good fighting fuck." He says as he begins dragging me behind him by my hair towards a door.

Pulling me inside, he slams the door shut then throws me onto a bed that stinks like old sweat.

I watch in horror as he pulls his shirt off tossing it away then grabs what looks like a police baton off the table in the room.

My eyes scan my surroundings, my eyes landing on the huge lamp next to the bed. As soon as he is close enough, I grab the lamp swinging with all I have.

It crashes across his head with a loud thump and I watch as he goes limp across the bed. Making a run for it, I get to the door, jerking it open only to run into a hard chest with an oaf.

"Well, you are most certainly a fighter." Grant murmurs to me as he twists my arms behind my back, tying them again.

He doesn't go to check on his creep friend, just closes the door back before leading me back to the room he had me in before.

Putting me back into the chair and making sure that I am secure, he walks over to the desk pulling out a huge hammer.

"Don't make me use this. Stay where I put you. Okay?" He asks calmly and I shiver.

Without another word, he leaves again. A few minutes later I hear yelling in the hallway just before there is a huge explosion that shakes the whole building. I smile. My man is coming.

Reaper

We unload at a dock going into the warehouse next door to the one the Abyss MC is holed up in. Buzz was able to find an old tunnel that went underneath the ground connecting the two.

Sneaking up into the warehouse from below was tricky, we were not sure where the leader of Abyss would have his guys stationed inside.

Lucky for us, they didn't seem to know the tunnel was there. Aero was in charge of rigging the bomb on the far side of the warehouse in hopes of tricking them into thinking that was the area we were coming from. So far, it looks like it worked.

Slowly making our way through, checking rooms as we go, we take a few of the stupid fucks down. We need to work quickly because with the bomb, someone would have called it in. We don't want to be caught here when the cops roll up.

As I come up a hallway with doors on both sides, I see another room at the far end with the door wide open.

Right in the middle of the room is my girl. The first thing that I notice is her face is bruised and beginning to swell. The anger inside, drops to my stomach at the thought of them touching her.

"Come on in Reaper my boy. I've been waiting for you." I hear another voice from inside.

Slowly entering, I come face to face with someone I thought I would never see again.

"Grant." I say through clenched teeth.

"Drop all the guns outside then shut the door behind you. Do it or I'll shoot her in the head." He says with his gun pointed right at Jade.

Not taking my eyes off of him, I drop all of my weapons outside before walking the rest of the way in and shutting the door.

"Even if you kill us both, you won't make it out of here alive. My guys will make sure of that." I growl at him.

Trying not to take my eyes off of him for too long, I glance at Jade.

"Baby, are you okay?" I ask her but she doesn't respond. "What did you do to her?" I grit out.

"I just put her to sleep. She's still breathing." He rolls his eyes like it's just a simple matter.

I slowly walk around the room trying to see a weak spot before I can take my chance to take him out. I'm trying to get his gun following me and off of Jade.

"Why are you doing this?" I ask.

"Because it all should have been mine. You fucked that up just like you fucked up the club." He looks at me with hate filled eyes.

"My dad thought you were his friend." I say.

"So you figured it out have you?" He says with a smile.

"I figured it out before you left, asshole. The night you ran should have been the last night you ever had on this Earth." I growl.

"Well tonight is your last instead. Goodbye Reaper." He smiles but just before he pulls the trigger another bang goes off shattering the very small vent window above the door.

I watch as he drops to the ground, gun clattering across the floor. Running over to him, I begin punching him in the face over and over.

I vaguely hear the door open and others running in before I am pulled off the fucker now bleeding all over the place.

"Reaper!" Grease shakes me until I look at him. "We have to go. Sirens in the distance."

"Is he fucking dead?" I ask, kicking the fucker on the floor.

"He's still breathing." Chucky says, checking for signs of life.

"Take Jade. I'll be right behind you." I murmur, pulling my large blade from my boot.

I watch as the guys pick up Jade and walk out of the door before I kneel down over Grant.

"Look at me you stupid fuck." I calmly say, slapping the flat side of my knife against his cheek.

His eyes barely open, looking right at me. He's already dying, most likely painfully as his life's blood seeps out across the floor.

"My face will be the last you see. When you get to hell, tell the devil that the Reaper sends his regards." I grin as I slowly push my blade into the middle of his eye all the way to his brain causing his body to convulse.

I wipe my knife off on his clothes, sticking it back into my boot, walking out with a smile on my face.

Catching up with the guys as they load back up into the trailer, I take Jade into my arms and try to wake her up.

"Is it done?" Grease asks quietly from beside me.

"It is done. My father and mother can rest now." I whisper back.

"Reaper?" Jade mumbles groggily.

"Yes, baby. I've got you. You are safe now." I kiss the top of her head as she tries to smile.

Her face is badly bruised and I am not yet certain what all she had to endure before I got there.

Chucky is currently on the phone with Maria making sure that she and Joanna are prepared to look over Jade when we get there. If she needs the hospital, Joanna has some friends in the emergency room that can make sure things remain quiet as to what went down.

Jade

When I wake up again, Joanna and Maria are there trying to clean me up. I talk them into helping me take a shower and feel better immediately after.

Looking in the mirror I can see how bruised my face is and know that it could scare the kids to see me this way but I still demand to be taken to them to see them for myself. I was so worried that they too were taken when I was.

"See, they are sound asleep." Reaper says from behind me. "You girls go get some rest. I'll take care of Jade for now." He whispers to Joanna and Maria.

"We'll check on you in the morning, Jade." Maria says softly, rubbing my upper arm. I give her a smile as they both walk away.

"Come on, you need some rest too." Reaper murmurs, sweeping me up into his arms.

"I can still walk, you know?" I smile into his face.

"I know. But I like having you in my arms." He smiles back, walking back into the room I was in earlier.

"We aren't taking up one of the other guys' rooms are we?" I ask as he lays me on the bed.

"This is actually my room the few times I've stayed here. The one the kids are in is normally used by prospects but we currently only have one of those at the moment." He strips down to his boxers, laying down next to me.

"What's his name?" I ask, laying my head on his arm.

"Who?" He grunts back.

"The prospect. What's his name?" I ask again.

"Prospect." He shrugs his shoulders seriously causing me to laugh.

"You guys never change." I shake my head.

"Until he earns the new road name we give him, that's his name. Prospect. It's the way the club works." He explains.

"I know but it still feels weird for me to call several people at a time, Prospect." I roll my eyes.

"The way I see it, it makes it easier. You yell Prospect and they all come running at once." He smiles down at me as I laugh out loud.

"Awful. Just awful." I huff back.

"But I'm your awful so it's all good." He says, making me laugh again.

"I love you, ya know? I always have." I whisper a few minutes later.

"I have always loved you too, even when you didn't know it." He whispers into my hair. Within minutes I am asleep, wrapped in the arms I should have always been in.

——

Chapter 11
Reaper

It took almost six months to get everything straightened out after the death of Brandi. I got custody of Cole because Brandi and I were still married when she died. Since she never named the real father, in the eyes of the law he is mine.

Jade jumped right to work about a week after the incident, calling doctors and specialists about Cole. She took him to dozens before a plan was put together to get him the help he really needed.

None of the doctors thought he was on the spectrum. He's just a child that's lived in fear. He doesn't need to live that way any more. And very slowly over the past year we have watched him come out of his shell.

"Daddy? Mommy says not to be late." Turning to the little voice behind me, I look at Cole as he walks towards me.

"Look at you! What a nice suit you are wearing. Grease help you with your tie?" I ask, kneeling down to look at him.

"Mommy." He says, shaking his head.

He still sometimes only responds with one word but he's definitely getting better with it.

"Guess, it's time to go get married then." I smile as Cole screws his face up. "Don't you want to be married one day?" I ask him.

"No." Is all he says before turning around and heading to the door. All I can do is laugh out loud at the look on his face.

"You'll change your mind one day." I say following him out the door.

"No, No, No." He repeats like a mantra and I laugh even harder.

Jade

"You look so beautiful! I think I'm going to cry!" Mina says looking over my shoulder.

"I'm so glad you and Timber could come." I say, looking back at her.

"I wouldn't have missed it for the world. Besides, Timber knew he could either bring me or I was coming by my damn self!" She shakes her head as I laugh at her so matter of fact statement.

"You are still the same as always. Poor Timber." Fire shakes her head at Mina.

"He knew what he was signing up for! And if he didn't, it's too late now." She points to their son while rubbing her pregnant belly.

"Well, are we ready to go girls?" Maria asks from the doorway.

"Are the guys already out there?" I look over to her.

"Yep and looking dashing as ever." She smiles back.

"Then let's get this done." I announce nervously.

"You look like you are going to throw up." Fire looks right at me, stopping me at the door.

"I can't remember my vows." I say back with wide eyes.

She starts laughing hysterically which pisses me off.

"Why are you laughing?" I demand.

"Because it would serve his ass right if you just stood there like a statue." She keeps laughing as she walks away.

"You are so fucking mean! I can't even understand how we are sisters!" I pick up the front of my dress, walking away from her laughter.

Grease

Watching my President of the club get married earlier to the woman he loves actually puts a smile on my face. Something that rarely happens these days.

I figure my marrying days have long since passed since I am turning forty-two this year. I am always too busy with work and helping to change the club over to more legal activities.

No one would want an old fucker like me anyways. I can't even imagine having kids now. Hell, I would be almost sixty before they got grown.

However, that doesn't mean that I don't still love a good romp in the sheets with a beautiful woman.

Walking around the reception at the clubhouse, I've spotted the one I want to hear screaming my name later.

She's fucking gorgeous in that simple way women sometimes have. I don't think she's even wearing makeup which in my opinion is a good thing. Most these women gob that shit on like a mask, so when you wake up next to them in the morning light you are asking yourself what the fuck you were thinking.

She has long gorgeous red hair that shines in the sunlight. She must have come straight here from work, she is wearing scrubs with a name tag.

She's currently talking to Jade who is standing next to Reaper, so I can use his ass as an excuse to get closer and at least find out her name.

As I walk up, it sounds like they are talking about Cole so this chick must work at the clinic where Jade takes the kids for check-ups.

Her eyes look over at me and then away before returning again. I give her my best smile as I look her up and down until Reaper elbows me in the ribs.

"Don't worry Britni, he may look intimidating but he's just a big teddy bear." Jade says while looking at me with slitted eyes.

"Name's Grease." I hold my hand out to her in which she takes it.

Her hands are soft just as I knew they would be from working in a doctor's office.

"Britni. It's nice to meet you." She introduces herself before pulling her hand away again.

I'm a little surprised to realize I miss the feeling of it in my own.

Britni

Coming to Jade's wedding and reception, I wasn't sure what to expect. We have all heard the rumors that circle around the Night Howler's club but I had promised I would be here as soon as I could get off work.

Jade and I became friends after she started bringing the kids into the clinic where I work. She's such a great mom to her kids I figured the club couldn't be that bad.

Everything was beautiful during the wedding and all the guys were very respectful towards me. It wasn't until I met Grease that I felt uncomfortable.

He looked at me as if he could already see my naked body underneath my scrubs. The feeling of his rough hand in my own when we met, sent chill bumps down my body causing my nipples to tingle.

He might be a little older than me but the man was hot as sin with eyes that made it even more scorching hot outside.

Even after talking to Jade while he just stood there staring at me, I could still feel his eyes on me as I walked around talking to the others.

I'm standing at the table to get a drink when I feel a body push into me from behind. I seem to already know who it is.

"Just grabbing a beer darling." He murmurs next to my ear, reaching across the table to grab a cold one from the iced down tub.

Not saying a word, I turn my head to look directly into his eyes. My breathing picks up and my body stands to attention as it notices the hardness of his pressing even more into me from behind.

Feeling bold. I press back into him with a small smile, lifting my eyebrow.

"How about we go somewhere a little more quiet so that I can hear every sigh that escapes that beautiful mouth before you scream my name." He whispers, running his tongue along the shell of my ear.

"Yes." Is all I breath out before he grabs my hand and pulls me with him across the yard stopping next to a huge bike.

Holding out a helmet, he waits to see if I take it before climbing on.

"Have you ever ridden before?" He asks.

"Not a bike." I state with a smile that makes him grin.

"Just climb on, put your feet on the pegs there and hold on tight." He grins back.

I put the helmet on and climb on, wrapping my arms around his waist. In just a few more minutes, we are flying down the road and I am loving every second of it.

The   End,   For   Now.

Sneak Peak
Night Howler's MC,
New Orleans, Book 1

Buzz

Several years ago, my little sister was raped and murdered. Her killer was never caught. She had been emailing a guy she had met in an online chat room. Even though the authorities had his name he used online, every lead came to a dead end. It didn't stop me from continuing the search.

A few weeks ago I caught a break. Another programmer I knew from when I was still in the service stumbled across the same name with a different unique IP address that constantly bounces around making it almost impossible to follow.

However, follow it I did and where it winds up leading me has me second guessing what I am planning.

I'll take something of his. His beautiful sister Markayla. But we don't hurt innocents. I will protect her as best I can. I plan on her step brother paying for what he did to my sister with his own blood. What I don't plan for is falling hard for my enemy's sister.

Even after all of these years I can't believe my mother was stupid enough to fall for my step father. I have never doubted he had something to do with her disappearance. I've just never been able to prove it.

You would think that with her gone, I'd be free of the Marcus family. Unfortunately for me, my step father adopted me when he married my mother.

My step brother absolutely hates me and I am certain that our Papa is the only one keeping him from doing whatever he wanted to me.

The look I see in his eyes any time I run into him while I am out with friends or a date scares me to my core. I refuse to let him know just how scared of him I really am.

If anything ever happens to Papa or I become expendable in his eyes, I will need to run and run fast. Getting away before he gives me to Joe to do whatever he wants with me, will take a miracle.

GET IT HERE:
https://books2read.com/BuzzNewOrleans

Chucky's Pride
A Night Howler's MC Story
Maria

Today is my first day back at work in over a month. I took an extended vacation just to get away for a while. The first week on vacation I stayed in Memphis with my best friend Rae. After all the nights spent trying to drink all the Jack Daniels in the area, I am completely surprised my liver is still working properly.

She and I spent most nights partying down on Beale Street, which is where I got my tongue pierced. I had said I was going to do it since my nineteenth birthday several months ago. At first having something like that in your mouth feels really weird, but then you get so used to it, and you forget it's even there. Well, except you find yourself twirling it around in your mouth constantly.

"Good God, I wish you'd stop doing that. It seriously looks like it would hurt," my aunt, and the boss, remarks as I walk in.

We all work in the family owned gas station. It's practically the only one in this little town. Aunt Joy is the manager, my mom is the assistant manager, and I work as a cashier. I have worked here for only about three years, but my mom and Aunt have been here longer.

"It doesn't hurt at all, Aunt Joy. You just don't like seeing it because you are a prude." I add as I stick my tongue out at her causing her to laugh.

"Kaye, can't you do something with your daughter?" she demands of my mom, who is busy stocking the shelves.

"She is twenty years old, Joy. I blame her father for the way that she is."

"You can't blame Daddy, Momma. I spent most of my childhood with you," I smile.

"Why would you get such a thing in your mouth anyway?" my mom asks.

"Because it makes *blowjobs* a little more interesting," I answer as I wag my eyebrows up and down in a suggestive way. My aunt wrinkles her nose and Mom just shakes her head and goes back to stocking the shelves. I just laugh as my Aunt Joy wrinkles her nose at me.

We hear a rumble from outside as a lone rider on a motorcycle pulls up to the gas pumps. From behind the counter, I watch as he gets off the bike and takes his helmet off. All the hair on my arms and neck stand on end as I watch him walk towards the door.

As he steps through the door, his eyes cut my way and just about suck all the air from my body. His blue eyes have me rooted to one spot.

"Bathroom?" he asks.

I vaguely hear my aunt answer his question as I am still standing there like a crazy person watching him stroll to the bathrooms.

My body has never acted like that just from looking at a man. I do have to admit that he is the most gorgeous man I have ever seen. There is just no way he's from around here. They don't grow them like that in Mississippi.

Hell, they don't grow them like that in Tennessee, either. I should know. I just spent most of my vacation there and not once found a guy that even remotely got a second look from me.

A few minutes later, he stands at the counter as I ring up the drinks and snacks he picked out.

I bite my tongue ring, swirling it outside my teeth without even paying attention. "You from around here?" I ask casually.

"I'm from all over really, but currently staying with some of my brothers on the other side of Tupelo. But, I'll be close by here for a few days. Don't know many people around here," he drawls as he looks up at me with a grin.

All I can think is, *Oh, fuck me. He has dimples.* I feel my nipples tightening up against my thin shirt, and I pray he can't see it through it.

"My name is Maria," I grin, "so now you know me. Would you like to get a drink Friday night? I know a really good bar we could go to," I add breathlessly.

"Sounds good to me," he tells me. "Everyone calls me Chucky." He holds his hand out to me palm up, and it takes me a minute to realize he wants my phone.

I watch as he calls himself and hands it back.

"I'll text ya about the details, beautiful." He grins at me as he takes his purchases and backs out the door, staring the whole way.

"Good lord, he sure was pretty. If only I were about thirty years younger," I hear from behind me.

"I thought Maria was going to pass out from the look on her face when she looked at him the first time. She didn't look like she was breathing." My mother jokes to my Aunt.

"She's still not talking, which is strange, should we check her pulse and make sure she is still alive?" asks my Aunt as I turn around to glare at them which doesn't stop them from laughing at my expense.

"Did you at least get his number?" mom finally asks.

"Better than that, I asked him out for a drink this Friday night." I finally smile wide at them both.

"Just don't do anything we wouldn't do." My aunt winks.

"Knowing you two, that doesn't leave a whole lot out." I laugh as they both huff and walk away.

I'll never get tired at riling the two of them up. For one, they make it entirely too easy to do. Even though they both love going out and having a good time, they are both still a little old fashioned about some things.

GET IT HERE:
https://books2read.com/ChuckysPride

Poison Pen
Baratta's Darkness

Baratta

The club is packed as I make my way to the balcony hoping to get some air. Finding a quiet spot on the far side, I sit and drink my scotch slowly while the boss finishes up his meeting inside. A few minutes goes by when a young woman walks out, stopping to look over the balcony to the street below. New Orleans is always a party town, especially on Saturday night.

She doesn't seem to notice me in the corner, but I happen to be good at blending into the shadows. My eyes are drawn to her, not just by her beauty but by the gorgeous tattoo that goes up one leg disappearing under her short skirt.

"Hey, we all are going to another local spot. Want to come with us?" I hear as another woman walks up next to her.

"Nah, I think I'll call it a night soon and go back to the hotel. My flight leaves pretty early." She responds in a sultry husky voice that immediately has me wondering what she would sound like with her legs wrapped around my head.

She stays in the exact same spot for several more minutes after the other girl leaves. As she turns around, she finally notices me as she jumps a little bit and her hand goes to her chest.

"I'm sorry. I didn't see you there." She smiles in my direction.

"I wasn't really trying to be seen." I respond as I take another sip of my scotch.

"Well, sorry." She says as she turns to leave.

"Where are you running off to?" I ask not really wanting her to leave which is completely out of character for me.

"Back to my hotel. I have an early flight." She smiles again and I catch my breath at her beauty yet again.

What the fuck is wrong with me? I think to myself. I am never impulsive. I calculate everything.

"So you are not from around here then?" I grin back at her as I lean forward, more into the light. I watch as her smile becomes even bigger. *Maybe I won't have to go very far for a fuck tonight after all.*

Fiona

Today was a huge success for my business. Accepting the invitation to the Inkers Expo they were holding this year in New Orleans was the best decision I could have made. There were so many big names in the business here that would be able to get my name out there. There were several reporters that stopped to take pictures and ask questions about my work.

My dreams were coming true and I had my brother to thank for that. He and his club, The Wolfsbane Ridge MC, gave me my first loan to open up shop after they realized how much I loved to draw and eventually do tattoos. I don't use stencils to do my work, everything is by hand.

Finished with cleanup at my station, I begin packing all of my supplies back into my duffle bags when a couple of the girls I met here walk up asking if I want to go to the after party with them. I think it would be fun, plus hopefully another chance to meet some more people in the business with connections.

"Whew! They are so packed tonight!" Lilyanna comments as we scan for an area to sit.

"Look, there's Clint with some of the others. Let's go up there." Ashley points to the balcony above where there are less people but more of the crowd from the Inkers Expo.

A couple hours later, I decide to get some air as I excuse myself from my friends and head outside. I look out over the street below at all people walking around and having fun. Some I know are tourists as they stop every so often to take pictures.

I haven't taken a single moment to do the tourist thing. I'm out of time now since I leave tomorrow. Hopefully I can come again just to visit and look around without worrying about work. I think to myself as I watch everyone below.

"Hey, we all are going to another local spot. Want to come with us?" asks Ashley as she comes up behind me.

"Nah, I think I'll call it a night soon and go back to the hotel. My flight leaves pretty early."

"Have a safe trip and don't forget about all your new friends now." She says with a smile.

I hug her as we say goodbye. Looking back out over the street below I think about all the new connections this week has brought me. I am truly excited to get back home and get started on all the new bookings I have for next week.

As I turn around a guy in the corner catches my eye and I jump a little not expecting to see anyone. *Has he been there the whole time?* I ask myself. GET IT HERE: https://books2read.com/BarattasDarkness

Blood

The first time I ever saw Miranda Grayson was in the parking lot of the grocery store. She had her arms full of grocery bags and was having a hard time opening the trunk of her car.

I walked right up, took the bags, opened her trunk, put everything in and walked away. Without every saying a single word. I remember looking back before getting on my bike and seeing a look on her face as if she thought I may be missing a few marbles in my head.

Currently, I'd say she was correct in her assessment. I can't seem to put together a complete sentence in her presence. I'm not sure why her presence has that reaction with me. Quite frankly it pisses me off. I'm not always sure if I want to kill something or just fuck her brains out.

Can you fuck someone until you get them out of your system? I'm not really sure but with her, I'd damn sure be willing to try. But I highly suspect after the first taste of her, I'd never let her go.

Miranda

I've been through hell over this past year but I refuse to allow it to destroy me. They took me from my own home and I am still unsure how exactly they got in. I've not stepped foot back in there since it happened.

Currently I am sharing a room in the Wolfsbane Ridge MC clubhouse with a gorgeous hulk of a man that has rarely spoken two words to me. I should be afraid of him just based on his size. But, oddly, I am comforted by his presence.

I'm sure he'll eventually want me to leave or at least move to a different room. Surely a man like him has a ton of women or maybe even a girlfriend. He wouldn't want to continue to take care of a woman like me. One that is so used up and completely broken.

Uncle John has been by several times already trying to get me to go back home with him. But I am not ready. Especially since he told me that Ray has been by looking for me.

I need to wait until I am stronger. That way I can run because I know if Ray catches me this time, he'll kill me.

GET IT HERE:
https://books2read.com/BloodsAngel

Sign Up for Marissa Ann's Newsletter
https://mailchi.mp/3ca12e9bcaec/1ex5ytjtmd

Connect with the Author

Facebook:
https://www.facebook.com/MarissaAnnAuthor
Instagram:
https://www.instagram.com/authormarissaann/
Twitter:
https://twitter.com/marissaannbooks
Goodreads:
https://www.goodreads.com/author/show/18159
855.Marissa_Ann
Linkedin:
https://www.linkedin.com/in/marissa-ann-
ballard-93982b186/

Other Titles by Marissa Ann
Wolfsbane Ridge MC Series
Book 1 Timber's Fairy
https://books2read.com/u/47lz7E

Book 2 Blade's Pixie
https://books2read.com/u/38RPla

Book 3 Blood's Angel
https://books2read.com/u/m2MnoG

Night Howler's MC, Mississippi
Book 1 Chucky's Pride
https://books2read.com/ChuckysPride

Book 2 Reaper's Jewels
https://books2read.com/ReapersJewels

Night Howler's MC Series, New Orleans
Book 1 Buzz
https://books2read.com/BuzzNewOrleans

Hearts of Steel Anthology featuring
Wolfsbane Ridge MC, Book 4 Wrench's
Salvation
https://books2read.com/Hearts-Of-Steel-
MC-Anthology

Poison Pen Series
Book 1 Baratta's Darkness
https://books2read.com/BarattasDarkness

Book 2 Lily's Shadow
https://books2read.com/LilysShadow

A Call Of Magic Limited Edition featuring
Hydra: The Dragon Keeper
https://books2read.com/callofmagic

Let's Play, A Limited Edition Sports Romance
Collection featuring:
All I've Got
https://books2read.com/letsplay

Sea's Of Rissa, a Collection of Poems
https://books2read.com/seasofrissa